"Harry Rubin's book, *Traitor's Revenge*, is a thriller that grabs ahold of a reader and won't let go until the book is finished. It's a highly effective dual narrative novel that connects characters in two very different times and places, with many twists and turns that keep the reader's attention until the climactic ending. It's a highly recommended reading adventure."

—WILLIAM MURPHY, Author of Not for *God and Country* and others

"Intriguing and clever. The author uses his experience and wit as he delves into the complicated lives of men that were created by the horrors of the Vietnam War—5 stars for never-ending suspense."

—DONALD J. "DJ" HUMPHREY II, Author of *8 Miraculous Months in the Malayan Jungle*

"Harry Rubin is a great American hero and utilizes his firsthand accounts in Vietnam to create an action-packed thriller in *Traitor's Revenge*."

—DANIEL "DOC" JACOBS, HM2(FMF), USN (RET), Bronze Star with Valor and Purple Heart, President and CEO Doc Jacobs Foundation

Traitor's Revenge

by Harry Rubin

© Copyright 2021 Harry Rubin

ISBN 978-1-64663-285-5

Published by

 köehlerbooks™

3705 Shore Drive
Virginia Beach, VA 23455
800-435-4811
www.koehlerbooks.com

TRAITOR'S REVENGE

A NOVEL

HARRY RUBIN

VIRGINIA BEACH
CAPE CHARLES

DEDICATION

Conscription in the United States, commonly known as the draft, has been employed by the federal government of the United States in six conflicts: the American Revolutionary War, the American Civil War, World War I, World War II, the Korean War, and the Vietnam War.

During the Vietnam war, over two million men were drafted for service there, and elsewhere, and for the most part stepped up to the plate and did the jobs they were trained for; some never came home. When I was in the hospital in Vietnam, I learned that most of the men there, though sick or wounded, would not trade the experience for anything.

It is to those men that accepted the responsibility thrust upon them and undertook the mission they were asked to do in the defense of their country that I dedicate this work.

CHAPTER 1

THAT COULD HAVE BEEN ME

The tear that dropped nearly froze on Hank Maples' cheek as he watched Ralph's casket lowered into the cold, hard ground. It almost seemed fitting that it should be this cold because Ralph was, indeed, a cold, hard man.

As Hank flicked the teardrop away, he looked around the gravesite to make sure no one saw his moment of weakness that took even him by surprise. After all that had happened over the years on Perkins Drive, Hank had become, to most, at least outwardly, the neighborhood tough guy, Ralph notwithstanding. Not many people knew Ralph, as evidenced by those in attendance at the burial. There weren't that many people at the funeral, and there were even fewer at the gravesite.

Perkins Drive was a cul-de-sac with fifteen modest homes and was bordered by two streets with much larger dwellings. Everyone on the street seemed to know one another, some intimately. Hank hadn't been home in many years but had kept up with the events around town by reading the local newspaper online. He wasn't sure why he continued to do that because he'd never planned to come back to the city of Atwood after what happened in 1963. But there he was, twenty years later.

Hank had seen Ralph's obituary in the paper and figured he owed him at least a visit to his funeral for what he did for him in their younger years, which included saving his life.

"Hank? Is that really you?" said a voice from behind him, followed by a tap on his shoulder. Hank turned and came face to face with his old girlfriend, Lacy Anderson, who looked great in her tight dress. Time had been very good to her. She sure didn't look the forty-five years he knew she was—they were the same age. He wondered what she thought of him.

"How are you, Lacy? It's been a long time. Eight years, maybe?"

She smiled in that alluring way she always had that suggested she was eager to one-up him. "I remember for sure, Hank. It's been twenty, because my nephew Joey was only one when you left in the middle of the night."

Hank hadn't actually left in the middle of the night, but he had left with haste. He knew at the time that she and Ralph were splitting up because she had desires that he didn't. Since he felt there was nothing for him in Atwood anyway and he wanted to avoid a confrontation with Ralph, he'd left rather quickly.

The rain and wind kept the graveside services short, and as soon as the preacher said the last prayer for Ralph, the few people gathered in the small graveside tent started to leave. Most of those that attended the funeral hadn't ventured to the cemetery because of the weather, and when the rain and wind that kept the service short started back up, those that did attend at graveside were eager to get to the reception at Ralph's mother's house.

Lacy asked in her daring way, "I hope you'll come to the house so we can talk for a while. It's so good to see you after all this time."

"I might stop by for a while, but only to give my regards to Molly before I get back on the road."

In truth, Hank was staying in Hargrove, the next town north, so he wouldn't have to be seen around town and answer all the questions that would likely be hard to answer truthfully. Not that he had too many secrets, but considering the business he was in, it benefited him to be as invisible as possible. When he returned from Vietnam—having been in the infantry and having led covert intel ops—he decided to continue that line of work and was hired to conduct high-stakes investigations that weren't always exactly above board.

Ralph's mother, Molly, was in her seventies, but like Lacy, she looked great for her age. She gave him a kiss on the cheek and a hug that to some would seem very suggestive.

"I am very sorry for your loss. I was always intrigued by Ralph's personality and graciousness," Hank said as she stepped back to gaze at him. He could see in her dark grey eyes that she was in pain at the loss of her only son.

"Hank Maples! It's good to see you after all these years. Hopefully, we'll get to see you more often. I just wish it were under different circumstances," Molly said as she continued to peer at him with an odd look in those piercing grey eyes.

Ralph had lived at 1134 Perkins Drive with his mother his entire life; she'd bought the house with her now-deceased husband many years ago. Hank didn't have the heart to tell her, but when this day was over, like twenty years ago, he planned to never return.

"Perhaps that will come to be, Molly. Again, I am sorry for your loss," Hank said. As he started to go back out the door, Lacy cornered him in the living room by the crackling fireplace.

"Not so fast, mister. I really want to talk to you, but this isn't the place. Can we meet somewhere later?" she said as she put her arm around his waist and gave him a slight hug. As she did so, her hip made contact with his, and he instantly felt a pang he hadn't felt in some time. He watched Molly mingle with the well-wishers until she walked into the kitchen out of sight.

"I'm not sure how long I'll be here and not so sure it would be a good idea anyway," Hank replied as Lacy let her grip on his waist go and turned to look at him face to face. At five foot eight, she almost matched his height. She looked fit and determined.

"Lacy, I sure would like to get together, but with all this going on, I'm sure Molly needs you to be close by. You're all she has now that Ralph has died," he said.

Lacy and Ralph never got married but had lived together since Joey was born almost sixteen years earlier.

"There are some things I need to tell you that you need to know, and since I've lost track of you, it may be that I won't get the chance again. So how about giving me a few minutes of your time?" She stepped closer and whispered, "I think it will be worth it, trust me."

Hank's heart raced, fueled by the perfume she was wearing. He would meet her, even though he knew things would end badly. Just like in the past, she knew she had him under her spell. They agreed to meet at Delaney's Pub at eight that night. Since it was only three thirty, he had time to visit with a few others from his past.

CHAPTER 2

TRUTH OR DARE

George Bandy lived across the street and caddy corner to Molly and Ralph. George was a good bit older but still recognizable. Like Molly and Lucy, he hadn't aged a bit, even though he was seventy. George had always considered himself the mentor of Perkins Drive, probably because he had lived there his whole life. He knew everyone and everything about them as well.

"Hank Maples? George Bandy. Remember me?" He reached out his thin hand to shake. "Haven't seen you for I bet years. How are you?"

Something bothered Hank about him as soon as he said hello. He didn't understand what it was or why but only knew it did. "I'm great, Mr. Bandy. Good to see you, and yes, it has been a while. You look great."

Mr. Bandy leaned a bit closer and said, "Too bad about Ralph, but when you burn both ends, sometimes you get caught in the middle."

Hank's interest was piqued very quickly. "I'm sorry, sir, but I'm not sure what you mean by that," he said.

It wasn't clear to Hank how Ralph had died. He presumed it must have been some sort of natural illness and hadn't thought to ask Lacy or anyone at the service. He leaned closer to him and said in an almost conspiratorial way, "Never a good idea to sell and use."

What? Ralph sold and used drugs? If that was the case, he'd never have guessed in a million years. The last time he'd read anything in the paper about Ralph, he was given the Citizen of the Year Award by the Atwood Chamber of Commerce for his continuous and ongoing support to the community through his auto dealership, which had turned out to be one of the biggest in the state. George must have seen his perplexed look.

"I know it's hard to believe, especially since you're not around here, but I can tell you lots if you would care to hear. If you do, let's get together and talk."

Great! Another meeting. His head was full of questions.

As George walked away, Hank watched a beautiful woman with two glasses of wine, one in each hand, approach. She smiled and offered one of the glasses to him.

"Well, I'll be damned, if it isn't Hank Maples. Have a glass of wine with me. I hate to drink alone."

Hank didn't drink much and had never been a fan of wine anyway. But who would refuse a drop-dead beauty with braided blond hair who was built for speed? He must have looked puzzled when she introduced herself as Claire Bandy, George's wife. She looked about thirty years younger than George, which made her about his age. *Trophy wife. Lucky George must have a game he plays that no one else can win!* Hank felt a bit awkward when she smiled, because she obviously knew what he was thinking.

"George and I have a unique arrangement," she said as he took a sip—or perhaps it was a gulp—of wine. "I've heard about you from George over the years and am glad to finally meet you. May I call you Hank?" she asked with a gleam in her eye. *Call me anything you'd like,* he thought.

"Of course, Mrs. Bandy," he said as she stepped even closer.

"Claire will do nicely," she said with a wink.

Trouble!

CHAPTER 3

DELANY'S PUB

Hank walked through the front door of Delany's Pub just before eight and spotted Lacy in the corner having a beer and a conversation with another woman he didn't recognize. She was beautiful as well with big grey-green eyes that seemed like they could pierce steel and a body that rivaled Lacy's. When he approached the table, Lacy said something to the woman, and she turned and walked away.

"Don't leave on my account," Hank said. The woman flashed an icy stare and walked off. "Damn, Lacy, what did you say to make her mad?" he asked.

"Nothing, really. I just told Missy that for now you were all mine."

"Lacy, first of all, I'm not anybody's and for sure not yours. I only came here tonight out of respect for Ralph, and you act like he has already blessed you with an excuse to do what you want."

"Sorry for the forwardness, but I know you're leaving soon, and there are some things you need to know now that Ralph is dead, things I didn't want to share with her."

Hank sat. As he did so, the waitress approached and took his drink order.

"So, what's so important?" he pressed, trying to avoid time-consuming small talk as the waitress returned almost immediately with a single malt scotch.

"For starters, you might as well know now that Ralph was no saint." She leaned closer and whispered, "It's not common knowledge and won't be, but Ralph committed suicide."

Hank was taken by surprise. Though he hadn't been back to Atwood for many years, it seemed as though Ralph had the world by a string and all that went with it.

"I don't believe it, Lacy. Why would Ralph do something that stupid with all he had going for him?"

"Well, you can believe it. All that you may think about him that made him so great was no more than a false front that had most people fooled. But I can tell you firsthand that he was deeply burdened by his past, and you were a big part of that past, Hank."

Hank thought back to the time just before he left town and wondered if what happened on a dark night twenty years ago had doomed Ralph. They'd been out drinking and had crashed into the side of another car that seemed to come out of nowhere. Hank remembered what happened after the crash, but most of the details had been blurred by the booze and the rest by time. He remembered that Ralph went to check on the other driver. Then, when he returned to the car, he'd said it was all okay and that they should return to town in their car and he'd get his tow truck and come get the other guy and his car. Hank got sobered up, returned to his house, and went to bed, his parents none the wiser. The next morning, he was gone, reporting to the military drafting station in Grove City, the next town over. From there, he was sent to Fort Gordon, Georgia, for basic training.

The engine was still warm, but the body not so much by the time the sheriff got to the wreck. A passerby had spotted the overturned car and called it in to Sheriff Tate. By the time the 911 call was routed to him, Tate was in a compromising situation with his girlfriend. As soon as he got to the scene of the wreckage, he was able to tell that the driver of the car in the ditch was dead. Sheriff Tate noticed that there was a piece of front bumper chrome from another car on the scene, and he was pretty sure he knew where that piece came from. It disappeared before anyone else arrived. He'd deal with the owner of the bumper piece in his own way. Sheriff Tate called the coroner and the only person in Atwood that had a wrecker to come and tow the car away.

When Ralph showed up with the wrecker, Tate called him aside. "I own you now," he said.

Lacy and Hank were just about to start what was to be an informative conversation when he looked up and saw Sheriff Tate walk their way, accompanied by Claire. *What?* Though Jimmy Tate was indeed the sheriff, he wasn't that much older than Lacy and Hank and, for that matter, Ralph as well.

"Well, I'll be damned. Aren't you Hank Maples?" he asked. Hank nodded, and the sheriff and Claire sat without being asked. *Shit!*

Tate never gave him a chance to answer his question before he asked another. "What brings you to town after all these years? Don't tell me it was Ralph's funeral. I thought you and Ralph parted ways many years ago." The sheriff glared into Hank's eyes. "I never had a chance to talk to you after that big wreck when the Clancy boy was killed."

"I'm not sure when that was, Sheriff Tate, but I would have had no information anyway. I don't mean to be rude, but Lacy and I have some catching up to do with little time to do it. Would you be offended if I asked you and Claire to please give us some privacy?"

Sheriff Tate gave Hank a wink, and he and Claire got up and went to the bar.

Hank's eyes followed them until they were seated. Tate's arm rested on Claire's shoulder as she snuggled close to him.

"What's that all about?" Hank asked Lacy, nodding toward the sheriff and Claire.

"That's one of the things I wanted to talk to you about. As I said, you really need to know what's going on here in Atwood if you really cared about Ralph, and it seems you do because you came home to his funeral."

He wasn't sure he cared that much, but he was starting to become curious as to what she had to say. There was a time when Ralph and Hank were pretty close, but they were also pretty young to have formed life-long bonds.

"I need you to promise that you won't repeat what I'm going to tell you to anyone, ever," Lacy said. Hank looked her in the eye and crossed his heart, promising not to. Her eyes turned dark as she leaned across the table. She cupped her hand around her mouth and said, "Tate is a murderer."

CHAPTER 4

YOU JUST THINK YOU KNOW

Jeff pulled into his garage, and as quickly as he entered, he shut the automatic closer. He'd watched his back window all the way home from the drop and was pretty sure he wasn't followed, but as always, he tried to take no chances. As soon as the garage door closed and he entered the house through the door into the kitchen, his cell rang. As he looked at the display screen, he realized that it would do no good to not answer because his boss had a visual on him coming and going.

"Yes?" he said as he went to the refrigerator and popped open a beer; he needed one after the night he'd just had.

"I assume all is well?"

"No problem, sir."

In truth, there were plenty of problems, not only with tonight's drop but with the entire situation. There were too many loose ends starting to develop, and every day Jeff seemed to be more in the middle than he liked. He'd made up his mind to get out of this situation as soon as he could.

"Sounds good," the voice on the other end of the cell said. "Keep up the good work. Your money will be in the same place in twenty minutes." At least Jeff could always count on quick pay for the work he did. There wasn't another job that could match what he made, and no taxes to boot.

Sheriff Tate looked over at his nightstand when he heard the vibration come from his cell. He kept it on vibrate to be discrete. When he saw the incoming number on the screen, he knew he'd have to take this call. He felt the other side of the bed; she was still there but fast asleep. The phone vibrated again, and Tate reached over and picked it up as he got out of bed and walked to the next room. It was just past three in the morning.

He answered, "Tate," so as to not let the caller know he already knew who it was via the saved number.

The familiar voice sounded tired and at the same time excited. "We have a problem that needs immediate attention. There is a loose end that you need to fix tonight."

This wasn't the first time Tate had been asked to fix a problem for the man on the other end of the line, and he would respond the same way he had for the last twenty years. "And that would be?" he asked.

The man explained that the drug drop this evening went a bit sideways and there needed to be an elimination, now.

"What's the big rush?" Tate asked, and as soon as he asked that question, he knew it was one time he would have been better off keeping his mouth shut.

"I don't pay you to think. Just do as I say and we will get along just fine. You understand, Sheriff?"

Silence.

It took a few seconds for Tate to respond, and before he could, there was a second, "Do you understand?"

Tate hated the situation he'd gotten himself into but could see no way out of it, at least for now. He hated this man—the husband of the woman he was having an affair with, a notorious prick named George Bandy.

"Yes, sir, no problem. Where will he be?"

"1143 Perkins Drive."

When Jeff returned from the drop-off spot, he smiled at the ease with which his life was going. He thought about the way things had been a few years back and knew that if not for this great turn of luck, he would be broke or dead. He never thought that he'd be involved in illegal drugs, but then again, after serving in the Army for almost four years and being dishonorably discharged for being AWOL for two weeks, he was left with little choice on the outside. In fact, because of what he did when AWOL, he was lucky he hadn't ended up in jail. So much for trying to pimp the three young women he'd met while on leave.

He unzipped the pouch and started to count the money inside. He smiled at the thousand dollars he had made tonight and opened the hidden compartment in the back of the closet where he kept his stash of money. A quick calculation on the scratchpad he kept inside with the money showed him that he had nearly forty-five thousand dollars. If he could stay out of harm's way for another three months, he would have enough to leave Atwood and start over somewhere else. Maybe find a few girls and start up what got him in trouble before.

He was a slow learner. He heard the floorboard creak and what sounded like a gun chambering a round but never heard the shot that ended his life.

CHAPTER 5

SPECIAL ASSIGNMENT

VIETNAM, 1967

"Maples, get your ass in here now," the major called as Hank entered headquarters back at base camp. When Major Barnett wanted something, he got it, whether he was right or wrong.

"Yes, sir," Hank said as he stepped through the door, came to attention, and saluted him.

"At ease, Maples," he said as he pointed to a seat across from his desk, indicating for Hank to sit. "I know you're infantry trained, but I need someone with a head like yours to get out in the forward area of An Khe, the home of the First Cavalry Division."

"And what would I do when I get there?" Hank asked.

Major Barnett pointed at the door with a wave of his hand; Hank could tell he wanted the privacy that closing it would give them.

"What you are about to hear is absolutely off the record, you understand?"

He gave Hank a look that said he'd regret it if he didn't give him the *yes, sir* he was looking for. Hank thought he was screwed no matter what he said.

"What will I be doing?" Hank asked in a way that told him he was all in.

"I'm getting reports of drugs in the field, and I need someone I can trust to find out the down low and the who," he said.

"Why me, sir? There is a whole company attached to this battalion that does that sort of thing."

"I don't trust a damn one of them, and they may all be involved as well."

Not being a trained investigator, Hank had no idea what to do and where to start, but the major made it clear that he thought he could get the results he wanted.

"There is a chopper waiting for you by the mess tent that will take you forward to An Khe, where you will be dropped off at HQ 510 and meet up with Sergeant Major Kelchner, who is privy to my plan and is expecting you."

"Yes, sir."

Hank never got to meet up with Kelchner; he was fragged the night before. Someone threw a grenade at him, and before he could react, he died instantly. Not a common occurrence in Vietnam but not unheard of, either.

Hank hung around HQ wondering what he should do and who he should contact. Major Barnett had said that Kelchner was his contact, and he wasn't sure who would be next in line for him to report to.

"Are you Maples?" a voice from behind him boomed. When Hank turned to answer, there was a lieutenant who looked about age twelve but with a scowl. His nametag said *Hanger,* and although younger than most non-commissioned officers, he would be tasked to lead in battle.

"Yes, sir," Hank replied and saluted. After a quick, casual salute back, he instructed Hank to follow him to his office in a crumbling structure that had been hastily put up when the first Cav made An Khe their division HQ.

"Have a seat, Sergeant," Hanger said, pointing to a seat next to his desk.

"Sir, I'm only a corporal. And I'm sorry, but I barely had time to catch my breath on return from the field when I was tasked to get on a chopper and come here to meet with Sergeant Kelchner."

The boy lieutenant shoved a piece of paper across the desk, and on it were two things. One was an official order that did indeed promote Hank to staff sergeant and another order that attached him to temporary duty to the HQ of the 12th Battalion of the First Cavalry Division effective immediately.

"Thank you, sir, but I will have to leave and get all my belongings and then come back," Hank said.

Hanger looked at him with an amused expression on his boy face and said, "Sergeant, no problem. All your stuff is already here. It followed you in the chopper that just landed."

"I appreciate the promotion, sir, but what am I being tasked to do? You know my MOS is Eleven Bravo, and this is a headquarters company." MOS was the identifier for one's training, and *Eleven Bravo* meant infantry. Hank had gone to jump school and had gotten the additional identifier of 1P, so his was *11B1P infantry paratrooper.*

"Major Barnett told me about you. He and I were tasked to handle the drug issue here in the First Cav."

Hank was a bit relieved to have at least what appeared to be a safe contact in base camp.

So had begun his new job of internal investigations.

CHAPTER 6

DELANEY'S PUB

"Tate is a murderer?" Hank repeated then asked what the hell Lacy was talking about.

"Do you remember the night Tom Clancy was killed in that car crash that never got solved? The hit-and-run?"

Hank wondered if she was asking because she knew he was with Ralph that night.

"I heard about it at the time, but if you remember, I got drafted and left the day after that and never heard anything about it since. Why do you ask?"

Hank was sure that no one knew that he was with Ralph that night, but maybe he was wrong.

"Tommy was a drug runner for someone getting a foothold here in Atwood, and the word around town was that whoever was in control here didn't want competition, so he made sure that he would have the area to himself."

Hank's mind drifted back to that night some thirty years ago, and he tried to remember what happened. It came to him that it was possible that Ralph knew where Clancy would be that night, and if Ralph was indeed working in the drug business, he could have intended to run into him—even with him in the car. He wondered, *Was I a fool back then, or is this just Lacy's imagination?*

"Are you trying to convince me that Ralph murdered Tom Clancy and then was able to cover all this up because he had a connection to Sheriff Tate? And why would Tate protect Ralph?"

"Hank, there is so much going on here now with drugs you wouldn't believe it," she offered, and he could only shake his head. "You were so unaware when you were eighteen. It was like your head was in the sand."

Maybe it was, Hank thought.

There was silence for a few moments before Lacy weighed in.

"When you were in Vietnam, what did you do?" she asked.

Hank wasn't sure how to answer. He'd been given a high security clearance in the Army and therefore couldn't really tell her the truth, so he made up a story that included combat missions and other jobs he had been tasked with before being tapped as an investigator.

"What makes you want to know what I did, Lacy? That was years ago, and I don't see why it would matter today."

"Let me be honest. I am a reporter for the *Herald* and am working on a story about the drug culture here in Atwood, and the entire county, that has persisted for decades.

"Hank, I know more about you than you know about yourself. And I think you'll want to help me with this investigation because you're in harm's way and don't know it."

"I have no idea what you're talking about. How could I be in harm's way here in Atwood? I've not been here in almost twenty years."

"If you come over to my house, we can talk in private. I'll explain what's happening and why you need to know."

His first thought was spending time alone with Lacy, as she'd told him earlier that she lived alone after her short marriage and quick divorce. She still had a body that many younger women would die for. Hank agreed, paid the tab, and they were headed for the door when Tate, who had been at the bar with Claire the entire time Lacy was filling him in, stood up and said, "Maples, you be sure and have a safe trip back where you came from."

"Thanks, Sheriff, but I might stick around for a short time." Hank surprised himself with his snarky comment.

"Then be sure to watch your back," Sheriff Tate sneered.

What's happening here? Shit!

CHAPTER 7

LACY'S HOUSE

Hank followed Lacy to her place on Perkins Drive, and when she cut the lights to her car and unlocked the door, he followed her into her modest home that mirrored the rest of them on the street where he'd grown up. Most were remodeled fifty-year-old homes now meticulously landscaped and maintained.

"Can I get you something to drink, Hank?" Lacy asked as she walked into the small but very nice kitchen and opened the refrigerator, pulling out a half-full bottle of white wine.

"No thanks, Lacy. I think I need to be on my toes and stay focused."

She sat on a chair next to a fireplace and motioned, with a provocative smile, for Hank to sit in the chair beside her.

"So what's so important that we have to discuss it in private?" he asked as she sipped her wine.

"First, Hank, I need to hear you tell me you won't repeat what I'm about to tell you, and I'll need to believe that you're sincere when you tell me that."

Hank nodded his consent.

Lacy said that she had no real proof of what she was about to tell him, but she was convinced that what she thought was going on was in fact very true based on events she was checking out and the mysterious ways of some of the leaders of the community. "Drugs are being imported from overseas in bulk and are being broken down into smaller amounts and distributed throughout the entire state. Here in Atwood, the use of drugs is starting to show up in every economic and social class." She paused and took another sip of her wine, looking in his eyes to gauge his reaction. Having spent the last fifteen years in the field investigating, Hank had gotten pretty good at hiding his emotions and remained stoic. She took another long swig of wine, as if working up the nerve to say something.

She didn't see any sign that he was impressed yet. She sort of pointed the wine glass at him and continued. "Hank, I think Sheriff Tate is close to the top of this operation. All I need is a few more pieces of the puzzle and a few more names of others involved to go to the federal prosecutor in Fairfax and get him to close this thing down. There have been several ODs in just the last few months here and close by that I think must be connected."

Hank still offered nothing in response to this information, although it made him rethink for a moment the way Tate had told him to watch his back. Lacy stood and set her glass down on the table, walked over to the fireplace, and stuck her hands out to warm them from the chill in the room. Just as she did, Hank heard a shot fired outside, and a bullet crashed through the front window, ripping into the wall just to the left of where Lacy was standing. He dove and pulled her to the ground just before a second and then a quick third round slammed into the same wall in almost the same spot. Whoever was firing the weapon was a very good shot, and Hank thought that from this point on he would carry his pistol at all times. Lucy was clearly becoming a threat to someone, and by extension, so was he. They lay there for what seemed like an eternity until they heard a car spin out on the street with the engine roaring as it sped away.

They jumped up and ran to the door, and as they opened it, many of the neighbors' porch lights began to come on. A few braver neighbors even opened their doors to see what was going on. Once out on the porch, Hank looked over at Lacy and was surprised to see she had a pistol in her hand; she looked comfortable with it.

"Shit, Lacy, what the hell just happened? And where in the hell did that gun come from so fast?" Not only did she give him an icy stare, but she poked him in the chest with the barrel of her sidearm and looked him dead in the eye.

"Now do you still think I'm full of shit, or are you going to try and help me get this drug issue solved? And just because you may have saved my ass in there, don't think I owe you one. I can protect myself."

Someone on the street must have called 911, because a minute later, Sheriff Tate pulled up in his unmarked cruiser, stopped a few feet from the front porch, and walked to where they were standing. It occurred to Hank that Tate sure got there remarkably quickly. Was he nearby at the time? Or, for that matter, maybe he was the shooter.

"Everyone okay? Anybody get shot?" he asked as he noticed the gun in Lacy's hand.

"Someone took a shot at my window. As a matter of fact, there were three shots fired, and none did any damage other than to my wall," Lacy answered and gave the sheriff a quizzical look as he gazed at her gun. "I'm sure you can check the records at the courthouse and see that I have a permit to carry, Sheriff. And you can be sure I know how to use it as well," she added in a challenging tone.

Based on what just happened and the fact Tate had told Hank to watch his back, Hank was beginning to think that instead of staying and helping Lacy, he needed to be on the road and never come back. Then again, it might already be too late. Tate looked at Hank and then at Lacy and said in a most intimidating way, "Not sure what the hell is going on here, but seems to me that when you two get together, bad shit happens. If I were either one of you, I would be very careful of what you do and say until we can figure out who shot up your place tonight, which might take a while. It seems no one saw anything, but we'll ask more questions in the morning."

With that said, Tate returned to his car, tipped his hat as if to say goodbye, and drove off into the night.

"Shit, Lacy, what have you gotten yourself into? And now it looks like you're dragging me in with you."

"Feel free to leave anytime you want, Hank. I can handle myself, as you can plainly see, and if you're not all in on this, I'd just as soon not have to carry your ass around if the going gets too tough."

Lacy looked at Hank with steel in her face, and it was right there, right then, he needed to make up his mind to either hear the rest of the story or get the hell out.

CHAPTER 8

COMPANY C

JULY 1967, VIETNAM

A little man on a motorized scooter pulled up in front of Lieutenant Hanger's office and quickly knocked on the door. Hanger looked up and motioned for the man to enter. As he did, he went to the window and appeared to be looking out to see if anyone had followed him or noticed that he'd entered the small office. Hanger motioned for the man to sit in a chair on the other side of the room.

"Maples, meet Duon Hong. Hong, this is Sergeant Maples. He'll be working with us now." The little man just nodded his head as if he understood but had nothing to add. "Hong is a trusted allied partner with ties to the Vietnamese growers here, and they trust him as well, so he's our go-between in our investigation."

Again, Hong nodded, and this time, Hank thought he saw a slight lift of his small chest at having been noted as an important part of whatever was happening. Maples thought Hong understood English, as each time Hanger said something, Hong's eyes moved with each word. "When is the next shipment, Hong?" asked Hanger.

Hong finally spoke up and in almost perfect English let them know that it was next week and added, "I think that the shipment will go through Bien Hoa at the base camp of the 173rd Airborne Brigade. There has to be someone who moves it to the airfield there, where it gets onto a military transport and is flown to the States. That is as far as I can seem to get."

Hanger asked Hong if there was a possibility of getting someone already on the base to help them, to which he said he could not, as the area was very well guarded, and the drugs only moved at night when there was even more security. When Hank asked what he could do to move forward with the investigation, Hanger looked at him and with a stiff stare said, "Maples, this is where you get to earn your stripes. The reason you were chosen is because of your jump status. You're being transferred to the 173rd as a squad leader in the Third Platoon Company C, which recently had some casualties. So it will seem natural that you would come in as a replacement. Once there, you'll keep on the lookout for any suspicious activity that would indicate drugs being moved onto or around the airfield."

Hanger added that Hank would report to him and only him either by phone or in person.

"Yes, sir," was all Maples could manage to say. Hank wasn't sure what Hong thought about him, but he had a bad feeling. As Hank saluted and turned to leave, a Jeep pulled up outside, and he was told by the driver to get in. He was off to the 173rd, which was only about twenty miles south down Highway 1.

Hank hopped out of the Jeep at Company C HQ and went in through the open doorway. He saw a makeshift desk staffed by a First Sergeant.

"Afternoon, First Sergeant. Sergeant Maples reporting for duty."

Hank handed him his service record folder and a copy of the orders sending him to the 173rd. He looked up at Hank, glanced at the order in his hand, and then opened the record folder and flipped a few pages down. He closed the folder and smacked it down on the desk, and with tired eyes he looked up.

"So what the fuck am I supposed to do with you here at Company C? I know you've been transferred here to be a squad leader, but from the looks of your recent post, you ain't qualified to lead shit down a latrine."

Hank looked at his name tag. "Sergeant Henry, I am only here because I was ordered to be here since there have been casualties, and you must be short on men to fill the gap. I have had training that will help me get the job done here. If you have doubts, I understand, and feel free to use me any way you want. I didn't come here to make trouble, just to get the job done."

"Okay, Maples. Get your ass down to the 3rd Platoon and report to Lieutenant Anderson. Let him know that you're a replacement for Decker."

"Decker?"

"Yeah, Decker. Took one in the chest last week. Had to send him down to *Vung Tau* to the hospital and never made it."

Lieutenant Anderson was lighting a cigar when Hank entered his command tent, and when he saluted and started to say, "Sergeant Maples reporting for duty," he waved him off.

"Enough of that shit, Sarge. Here on the front lines, we're all the same. Just be aware of the pecking order when it comes to orders. Here we are one big happy family most of the time."

"Thank you, sir, and you can be sure there is nobody more grateful for that attitude than me. Just let me know what you want me to do and where to go."

"You will be in charge of the 3rd Platoon now that Decker bought it last week. I know you were to be only a squad leader, but your rank puts you in charge of the entire platoon. You'll find some great guys eager to help you get adjusted and settled in. They're out on perimeter guard, so get out there, and they'll show you what they're tasked with and make sure you understand the front and the back of a claymore so we don't have to replace you as well."

The 3rd Platoon was on duty at the outpost in section four, protecting the airfield from attack by the Viet Cong and, for that matter, the NVA as well. The North Vietnamese Army was working the area, but the threat was mostly from the Viet Cong. The perimeter was defended by the 173rd, which used, among other items of defense, claymore mines that could take out anyone in its field of spray, about forty feet wide.

Duty at the front in daytime was actually a piece of cake, and most of Hank's new men enjoyed time there because of the less violent circumstances. But they also knew they'd have to take their turn at night. It occurred to Hank that during the day would be a good time to move drugs because of the relaxed atmosphere of the guards. He made a mental note to discuss this with Hanger.

CHAPTER 9

THE SLEEPOVER

So much had happened that day, Hank hadn't had time to find a place to stay in Atwood, partially because he didn't plan to be in Atwood overnight. By the time Sheriff Tate left Lacy's house, Hank had used some plywood he found around her house to board up the window that was shattered by the shooting, it was getting late, and he didn't want to drive the ninety minutes it would take to get to Hargrove. Lacy read his mind.

"Thanks for the help with the window. Since it's so late, would you care to stay here tonight?"

Hank blushed and paused, trying to think this through. Staying the night was as far from his mind as anything could be, and the question took him by surprise.

Lacy added, "What's the matter, Hank? Afraid of yourself, or are you afraid of me?"

Still a bit shaken up by the question, he wasn't sure what he wanted to do.

"You said you just got here today, and because of the time, you won't be able to get a room here on short notice," Lacy said.

Hank had a room seventy-five miles up the road in Hargrove, but he was tired and didn't feel like driving so late.

On the other hand, looking at Lacy and now realizing that she was all the woman any man could want, he thought it might be a very interesting evening. "Well, if you don't think it would put you out any, that couch over there looks pretty good right now," he said as he looked around at the mess on the floor that was still there from the shooting. "I could help you get the rest of this mess cleaned up and then get some rest and head out tomorrow."

Though his interest in this investigation was surging, Hank was debating whether to leave town or to help Lacy get the answers she was looking for. Getting shot at had pissed him off rather than deterred him.

"That works for me, Hank. I'll get some blankets and a pillow for the couch. By the way, it's a pull-out that turns into a bed, so it'll be more than comfortable for you."

Room enough for two, he thought as he watched her go to the other end of the house and return with a blanket and a large pillow.

"Let's clean up the rest of this mess before we pull out the couch so it'll give us more room to work," he said.

"Fine. I feel like we need a drink, so you clean and I'll fix something for us. What's your pleasure?" she asked and then remembered the Scotch from Delany's. "Dewar's okay?" He gave her a thumbs up and a smile.

Once the mess was cleaned up and taken to the trash out back, they sat in the chairs by the fireplace where they had started more than an hour earlier. After a rather long pull of Scotch, Lacy—now with a new glass of wine—broke the awkward silence.

"Hank, this is like old times for me, but just twenty-five years later."

The scotch on an empty stomach had already started to give Hank a slight buzz; Lacy looked even better than she had only a few hours ago.

"I guess you're somewhat right, but I don't think I remember being shot at whenever we were together then."

It had been over twenty years since his return from Vietnam. That was the last time he had been shot at, keyword "at" and not "shot."

"First time for everything," Lacy said as she came over to his chair and tipped her wine glass at him, to which he raised his glass and clinked his with hers. At the time, Hank wasn't sure what she actually meant by *first time* for everything, but some unusual ideas were stirring in his head. She returned from the kitchen with the bottle of Dewar's and without asking topped off Hank's glass then poured herself a bit more wine. After some small talk about the events of the night, Lacy returned to the chair she was sitting in prior to the shooting and relaxed and smiled at Hank with eyes that looked deep and almost black with a hint of want in them.

CHAPTER 10

PERIMETER GUARD

BIEN HOA, VIETNAM, 1967

Hank watched as the Huey dropped from the sky far outside the range of the claymores that were ready to blast to pieces anyone or, for that matter, almost anything in its destructive path. As the rotors began to slow, several men jumped to the ground around the chopper and spread out in what looked like a defensive formation, which from experience indicated that someone else of greater importance was about to get off as well. Several others got off, then in amazement Hank watched as Lieutenant Hanger got off, followed closely by Duon Hong, and then both Vietnamese and American troops. What little Hank knew about the relationship between Hong and Hanger and the drugs flowing in was about to change, and not for the better.

Prompting for the password to go past the perimeter guards, Hanger answered the question that made the difference between entering and death; there was no other alternative. Either pass the question or die at this line in the sand! Hanger was waved through the trip wires, walked to where Hank was standing with his M16 over his shoulder, and without a salute motioned for him to follow.

Not wanting to leave his command unattended, Hank motioned to Sergeant Ames to take his spot and instructed him to be sure to come get him if anything went wrong.

"Ames, I'll be in the command bunker for a few. Make sure the guys are at the ready if things turn bad. Remember, it's better to be safe than sorry."

Once in the fortified bunker, Hanger sat in one of the two rickety chairs and motioned Hank to sit in the other. Hong stood behind him and as usual had a look in his dark eyes that gave assurance that he wasn't only staying in the background but at the same time was keenly alert to the situation at hand. He too had an M16 slung around his back and was also armed with several US-made grenades and a standard issue .45-caliber sidearm. He looked like he was well suited to use them all and use them well.

On the surface, Hong appeared to be legit, but Hank remained suspicious.

"Maples, we have info that tells us that the next shipment from up north near Bon Song is on its way here and should be here in the next few days. Hong and his men will stay here and help intercept the shipment," Hanger said. "You and the Third Platoon will engage the Viet Cong that are bringing the drugs down. Hong will be their contact here, and if all goes well, we should not only have the drugs but capture those VC that are bringing it in. They think Hong is a middleman and will turn the drugs over to him."

"Sounds too good to be true. So if things don't go as planned, what are my plan B orders?"

"There will be no prisoners and no record of this engagement, understand?"

Maples understood and quickly answered, "Yes, sir, very clearly."

Hanger started back to the chopper, and as soon as the pilot saw him approach, the engine started to whine as the props started their slow turn until, at full speed, Hanger hopped on and the Huey lifted off, turning south and heading back to An Kea.

Hong spoke first and in almost perfect English. "Do you not trust me, Sergeant? You seem to hold yourself at arm's length when I am around you."

"No need to wonder, Hong. Let's just get this over with."

Deep in the jungle around Bong Son in south central Vietnam, a shipment of drugs was being broken down from bulk to more manageable smaller packages, and as the small Vietnamese workers went about their jobs, a large American was yelling at them to work faster. He fired a few rounds into the air for emphasis and yelled a few choice words in Vietnamese, telling them that the next shots fired wouldn't miss and someone's day would end early and not in a good way.

Private Ronald Evers was officially listed by the United States Army as missing in action. Actually, the only thing missing about Evers were his morals and his allegiance to the USA. Drafted in 1965 when he dropped out of high school, Evers never wanted to be in the service, and when the opportunity presented itself on patrol in the jungles of 'Nam, he took off during an ambush. When he found he was the last man standing, he headed north to enemy territory, where he turned himself in to the Viet Cong. From that point on, he was able to convince the small group of war-weary Viet Cong soldiers that there was a way to end their misery by selling drugs to the Americans. "Let them kill themselves with the drugs, a win-win for all," he said.

Time was getting short now, and he knew there were pressures from Army command to find the source of the drugs and shut it down. He could sense what was going on in the Army's effort to end the drug use in Vietnam by the trouble he seemed to be having getting the flow of his drugs to the end users. Everything seemed to take longer these days, and that could only mean the game would have to be shut down soon or he'd risk being captured by the Army and jailed as a traitor. If the Viet Cong saw his weakness and turned him over to the North Vietnamese Army, the NVA would use him for bait in trading for captured fighters. Or maybe just kill him for fun. Evers needed only one more score and he'd be set for life. He'd disappear to some remote spot in the world and live like a king, maybe even with a few queens to keep him happy.

CHAPTER 11

THE MORNING AFTER

"Hank, wake up!"

His head was throbbing like someone had hit him with a brick. Lacy stood over him with not much on other than a smile, a cup of steaming coffee in her hand. He wasn't sure what time it was, but he could see through the remaining window in the living room that the sun was coming up and there were slight wisps of clouds in the sky as if it was just about dawn.

"Christ, Lacy! What the hell happened last night?"

He looked around. Through foggy eyes, he could see the empty bottle of Dewar's on the table in the kitchen alongside the empty bottle of wine. There was also an empty pizza box with the name Delaney's Pub on it. He was on the floor in front of the couch he was supposed to have slept on that night, but it wasn't pulled out. He had either fallen asleep or passed out before he had a chance to do so.

"Don't tell me you don't remember the best part of the evening," Lacy said as she bent down to give him a hand up from the floor. "Maybe it was your lucky night, and maybe it wasn't. I guess if you don't know, you never will, because big girls don't tell," she said with a seductive smile.

"I need to go out to my car and get my shaving gear. And if you don't care, I'd like to get cleaned up and get my head together." She laughed. "What's so goddamn funny?" he asked as he started headed for the door to get his things out of the car.

"You look like shit, that's what's so funny. And if you could see the look on your face, you might laugh, too. Go take your shower and clear your head, and then we might talk about last night," she said as he unlocked the door to go to his car.

In the bathroom, Hank turned the water in the shower on as hot as he could stand it and stood there letting the steam ease his headache. He had his eyes closed, taking in the warmth of the water, when the shower curtain opened, and there stood Lacy as naked as him.

"Want company?" she asked as she entered the shower. "I want a rerun."

Now he knew what happened last night.

After several hours making love, talking, and getting to know each other again after him being away for some twenty years, it was starting to seem that this was always meant to be. They had been close in the 1960s—but not this close.

"Listen, Hank, as much as this feels right, don't think you owe me anything. I wanted this as much or more than you did, so if you need to pack up and go on your way, do so. I won't think any less of you." Lacy gave him a quick kiss on the cheek and brushed her hair back with the back of her hand at the same time.

He was still a bit confused about his feelings for Lacy, or more importantly, what he wanted to do about whatever they were.

"Let me make breakfast and we can talk about what might be next not only for our relationship, but also in this investigation," Lacy said. They both got off the bed, got dressed, and headed for the kitchen, where she started getting out the pots and pans and began cooking eggs, bacon, and toast. The smell of all that food did nothing for his stomach, which was still rolling from last night.

Breakfast hit the spot, and the hot black coffee started to bring Hank's senses back to reality. Lacy took the lead and point blank asked, "So, Hank, you in or out?"

"If you mean building our relationship, I really don't know. But if you want me to help your investigation of the drugs in this city, I'm all in."

"I told you our relationship is strictly up to you. As I said, feel free to pack and leave. But I sure could use your insight and experience to help me solve this drug investigation." She looked at him with her mesmerizing stare.

"Lacy, I'm all in!" He was still thinking about last night and this morning when he gave her his answer. So much for being cautious and watching his back like Sheriff Tate had suggested last night.

"Thanks, Hank. If you want to, you can get a room in town at the Twins Hotel. Or you can be my guest and stay here."

As casually as he could say it, he said, "With the shooting last night, it might be safer for you if I stayed here."

As soon as he said that, he knew it was the wrong thing to say. He remembered how quickly Lacy had had a gun in her hand after the shooting, and he knew he'd given the wrong reason. In truth, he was hoping for a repeat of the great time they'd had in her bed and hoped to be as lucky in the coming days—or, maybe given the circumstances, in the weeks—to come.

"Fuck you, Hank, if you think I need a babysitter. Get the hell out now and don't let the door hit your ass." Then her tone softened a bit. "If you want to help solve this shit, I'm sure we can get this done together."

"Sounds great. Sorry if I offended you. I know you can fend for yourself. I was just trying to be helpful. I only wanted to be by your side no matter what comes our way."

"Great," she offered and told him to take the guest room at the end of the hall. As he grabbed his bags, he got the impression that she was as excited about this arrangement as he was.

Later, they sat by the fireplace, which was still radiating heat from the embers from the previous night. He put another log on, and soon, the flames rekindled, and warmth filled what had been an icy room.

Wanting to take the lead in the conversation, Hank asked Lacy what she could prove regarding her suspicions and what she thought. She opened a large, note-filled file case and motioned for him to follow her into the kitchen. Once there, she spread out several articles across the table, ones not only from her newspaper, but several others in the surrounding area.

"Take a look at these articles and tell me what you see as a common theme."

While he read them, which took almost forty minutes, Lacy turned on her laptop. Whatever she was researching must have been exciting, because every few minutes, she whispered to herself, "I'll be damned."

After reading all the material Lacy had given him, Hank sat back and closed his eyes, digesting the information from the news articles and Lacy's handwritten notes.

"So, what do you think about all that you've read there, Hank?" Lacy asked.

"From what I can determine, there must be some local connection between the drug dealers and the users that never seems to get prosecuted," he answered.

When he looked at her, there was a smile on her face, and she simply said, "Bingo!"

CHAPTER 12

BETRAYAL

VIETNAM, 1967

Hong said he would be gone for a few days to help set up the trap for intercepting the next shipment from Bon Song.

"It will take a few days to get everything in place. When it's all set, I'll get on the radio and let you know how it will go down," Hong told Hank as he hopped in the front of a deuce-and-a-half truck that was headed to Bong Son hauling a five hundred–gallon rubber bladder full of aviation fuel for the choppers of the 1st Cav. There were ten trucks in the convoy, and they would have air support from the Cav in case of attack. With a lucky shot, a Viet Cong sniper could blow up the fuel and the truck—and the driver and the extra soldier riding shotgun. Still not trusting Hong, Hank made sure that the driver, Spec. 5 Herm Dover, was informed of his suspicions about Hong and would report anything he thought seemed odd about what Hong was doing and who he was seeing to him. They formed a code that would hide the true meaning of the message if intercepted.

Fifteen minutes into the trip, the first truck took on fire from the hillside, and one of the bladders exploded, instantly killing the driver and the door gunner as well. Although too late to do anything about the truck already hit, the three Hueys hovered in support of the now nine-truck convoy nosing down to the hillside where the Viet Cong were firing from. Within three minutes, there was nothing left of the ambush party that would be recognizable and not enough pieces left of them for any possible survivors to worry about burying. But because of all the trouble on the highway, the convoy was held up and would have to spend the night in Bong Son rather than return to Bien Hoa. Normally on a fueling mission, the convoy would drop its load and turn around and drive back empty to the base camp at Bien Hoa and then do the same thing the next day.

Dover and Hong went to the mess tent to get something to eat. After filling up on mystery meat, potatoes, and warm beer, they headed for a tent they would be sleeping in that night that the 1st Cav had set up for just such occasions. Tired from the grueling day on the road, they claimed cots at the end of the tent, said good night, rolled over, and quickly dozed off. About an hour later, Hong looked over at Dover, who was snoring, and went outside the tent into the night air.

Hong lit a smoke and quickly took three quick puffs, then three more. Evers saw the signal from the cigarette glow and quickly did the same to his own smoke. Hong, who was looking for the counter signal, took three more quick puffs on the cigarette and headed in the direction of the red glow he had seen.

Evers was waiting for him with three other men, all of whom were Vietnamese and heavily armed with AK47 assault rifles, pistols, and machetes. Evers was holding an M16 that he must have retained when he fled to the north. Hong was unarmed and understood that this wouldn't be a good time to screw up.

"Those god damned choppers made shit out of some of my friends up on the hillside," Evers said. "Lucky for you we knew which truck you would be in or this conversation wouldn't be taking place."

"Yeah, and if we weren't having this conversation, you could take the shit you have and stick it up your ass or give it to the gooks you work with and let them get shit-faced on it," Hong said. As he spoke, the three men with Evers gave Hong a stare and raised their weapons. They understood just enough English to know an insult when they heard one.

"Easy, guys, he's just a bit hot headed. We still need him to keep this deal together," Evers said. He waved his hand to the men to lower their weapons. Evers had always been amazed at the way Hong spoke near-perfect English, and though he never asked him, he thought that Hong must have been either born in America or somehow went to school there.

"Is everything all set for the drop?" Hong asked as he looked back towards the tent he'd come from to make sure he wasn't followed.

Evers looked around again and, seeing no one, let Hong know it was. "We have a half ton of marijuana broken down into two hundred five-pound bags that will make it easy to carry and hide at the same time," he said. "And I assume you have the money."

"We have one problem that we need to take care of when you and your men get to Bien Hoa with the weed," Hong said.

"And what would that be?" Evers asked.

"There is a new sergeant down there investigating this drug activity. He's starting to know too much, so we need to take him out as soon as possible. His name is Hank Maples, and he's working with command in An Khe. He's getting close to exposing our efforts."

"And you know this how?" Evers asked.

"Good news there. He thinks I'm working for the command as well as an advisor and interpreter. That dumbass Major Barnett at command thinks I can do no wrong. What an idiot. And to think he's West Point."

Evers smiled a freakish grin and asked Hong how he wanted to go about getting rid of the problem.

"They trust me. I'll be letting them know exactly when and where the exchange will be made and who to look for. You send the goods into the fake drop zone, and when you see him with me, shoot him and then drop the stuff fifty yards down at the real DZ. I'll meet you there with your money."

"And what happens to you in all of this?" Evers asked.

"I'll return to the fake site and fire off a few rounds as if I was protecting him. Command will understand I did what I could, and unfortunately, Maples will be dead. And as they say, dead men tell no lies—or in this case, the truth," Hong said and looked at Evers, who still had a smile on his face.

CHAPTER 13

NOT MAKING FRIENDS

N ow hooked on the situation and desiring to help Lacy find the truth, Hank committed himself fully to the investigation. Being the stubborn man he was, he decided to butt heads with Sheriff Tate and called him to see if they could get together soon for a short meeting.

"Sheriff Tate, Hank Maples here. I'm wondering if I could have a few minutes of your time sometime today?"

"What's on your mind? I thought you were just passing through after Ralph's funeral," Tate said.

Hank sensed a terse tone in his voice. "I wanted to ask a few questions about my old friend Ralph," he said. "You know we were pretty close back in the day, and as a matter of fact, I remember you and Ralph were pretty close as well."

"Let me check my calendar, and I'll call you back," Sheriff Tate offered.

After Sheriff Tate hung up, he immediately dialed another number. The man he'd called answered the phone on the first ring.

"Yes."

"Sir, I think we have a problem," Sheriff Tate told him.

"If there's a problem, it's not ours. It's yours. I don't pay you to get me involved. I pay you to do what needs to be done and keep me out of the loop," the man said and added just as quickly, "You do understand that, don't you, Sheriff?"

"I do, but Maples seems intent on getting involved with that bitch Lacy and her damn newspaper. I've checked him out, and he's no lightweight when it comes to sticking his nose where it doesn't belong. He runs a private investigation firm and is well connected because of his time in Vietnam. He's going to be a problem," Tate said.

With a tone that was as crisp as a cold winter day, the man simply said, "Then handle it."

Tate hung up and dialed Hank back, telling him he'd checked his calendar and had some free time around five o'clock in the afternoon. He could meet anywhere Hank wanted other than his office. He felt the need to meet more or less in a covert way so as not to involve any of the deputies that might be in and out of the office. He suggested they meet behind Delany's Pub around four-thirty that afternoon.

Hank hung up and looked at Lacy, who was listening on the extension and who gave him an odd smile.

"What's behind Delany's?" he asked.

She thought for a minute then told him there was nothing there but the parking lot for the downtown and an old garage that was used for parking and storage by the sheriff's office. Hank decided to go there early to make sure there were no surprises waiting; he would take his sidearm with him as well.

"I'll drive you there and wait for you in the pub. You can fill me in on what you and Tate talked about afterward," Lacy said. "I don't trust Tate any farther than I can throw him."

"That's not going to happen," he told her. "I'm going to just talk to him about how Ralph died and see if he can shed some light as to why Ralph committed suicide—if he actually did."

Hank got there early, as planned, and took a good look around. The parking lot was about half full and the garage was locked, but the windows were clear, and he got a good look inside. All that he saw were four parked cars.

He waited on a bench outside the building. His gut instinct, honed in Vietnam, was telling him not to trust the sheriff no matter where this conversation went, and he figured Tate felt the same. He watched as Tate's unmarked patrol car entered the lot, his sense of danger on high alert. Tate parked the car directly across from where Hank was sitting.

Tate put the car in park and opened the driver's side door, gave Hank a wave with his gloved left hand, and indicated with his right he was talking on his cell. As he approached the bench, Hank could hear him say, "I understand, sir, and please remember you don't have to call me about every little issue. I can fix these things for myself."

Hank thought back to the other night when he and Lacy had been shot at and wondered just what he was trying to fix. Tate approached and sat on the end of the bench, turned, and without any hesitation or small talk simply said, "What's so important that we have to meet like this? And why are you still in town?"

"Sheriff, I think I'm going to stick around here for a few weeks and help figure out a few problems that Lacy is working on. With my background, I might be a big help to her."

Tate listened carefully and then asked why Hank was revealing his intentions. "What makes you think I am interested in anything you might have to offer?" he said, giving Hank a menacing look.

"I thought since I'd be here, we should get to know one another and let me help you solve the drug issue around here."

"First of all, I know all I want to know about you. Secondly, my department needs no outside help, especially from you." Tate stood to leave. "As I said the other night, Maples, watch your back."

Hank watched the sheriff return to his car, and as he did, he could see him making another call on his cell. *I sure would like to know who he called,* he thought as he left the parking lot. Hank didn't think it would go this badly and knew he'd made no friend in Sheriff Tate.

CHAPTER 14

THE KILLING GROUND

VIETNAM, 1967

Back at base camp, Hank met with Lieutenant Hanger and Hong.
"What have you got for me? It better be good," Hanger said.
He turned to Hong and added, "Did you find your contact?"

It still puzzled Hank just what Hong's status was with the lieutenant. Even more confusing was his relationship with the Army. He wore civilian clothing, just like the rest of the peasants in all the villages throughout Vietnam; the only thing that was for sure was he had the trust of the company commander and, by association, Hank as well, though he wasn't as convinced as Hanger was.

Hong spoke before Hank had a chance to answer Hanger's first question. "Yes, sir. I contacted the seller, and I think he has trust in me," Hong said, adding that he thought the forty thousand dollars he promised the seller was adding trust as well. "When will I have the money to pay off the seller?"

Hong's demand for money raised a red flag with Hank. "Lieutenant, where is this money coming from? I think it'd be safer if I was in charge of the cash so if there's a problem with the transfer, it will be up to me to make sure the money gets back to where it belongs."

Hong smiled and added that that would be just fine with him. He realized his plan was going to work even better now that Hank had committed to attending the meeting where money was going to be swapped for drugs. If Hank was shot at the meeting, he would be listed as KIA, and there would be no questions about what happened because there would be no witnesses. Hong's word would be good as gold because of his relationship with the commander.

Back in the jungle, Evers was making sure that his men were aware of the target and the place for the swap. To make his men happy, Evers allowed them to smoke some of the MJ he was going to sell that night. The buyers wouldn't miss a few ounces, he reasoned. If all went well, Evers and his crew would end the rendezvous at Bon Son with both the cash and the dope. Evers had sold marijuana before but not nearly this much at one time.

Evers was on his field phone, lowering his voice so as not to be overheard by any of his workers.

"We are set to go at eleven hundred hours tonight," Hong told him over the phone. "Be at the coordinates I gave you the other day. And just so you know, Maples will have the money, so be sure you get a good clean shot that will take him out quickly. I'll be there beside him, so make sure you get him with the first shot. I want to see his face when he realizes that he has been played for a fool. Maybe if we're lucky, Hanger will come out of hiding and we can kill him as well."

Hong had asked Lieutenant Hanger if he wanted to be in on the capture of the marijuana and the seller. He knew these officer types and figured Hanger would want to take credit for the effort, anything for a promotion. *Two birds with one stone,* Hong thought.

As Evers was getting ready for the big night ahead, he sat back and thought about his past. He thought about the beatings that his father had given him almost every week and the fact that his slut mother gave him little comfort because she was either drunk or high on whatever drug she happened to be on at the time. He even tried to rationalize it all by thinking that as bad as his parents were, they were both victims.

Evers remembered the night when he was seventeen that his father, such as he was, came home around midnight drunk and staggering. When Evers was asked what time his mother got in and had to tell his dad that she wasn't home yet, he blamed Evers and tried to beat him. Evers ducked just as good old dad tried to sucker punch him. Evers responded quickly and punched his father's face, knocking him out. That was the last time he ever saw his dad.

His mother rolled in around three in the morning and was too drunk or high to realize that her prick husband was still out cold. Evers was gone and never returned. To survive, he became a drug dealer.

What a great life for a seventeen-year-old! He tried to find it in himself to excuse them for their lack of parental skills. He tried to find other reasons that he'd turned out the way he had, but no matter how hard he tried, he still blamed them for the way he'd been living his life to this point. It was no wonder to him then that he had such little respect for the system he grew up in and was proud of the fact that he was about to get his piece of the pie. With the two hundred thousand dollars he had accumulated from the past drug deals and now getting another forty thousand tonight, he would be set for the rest of his life as he saw it. His only disappointment was that he wouldn't be able to let his parents know that despite their failure, their neglected and abused son became financially successful and would soon live like a king, even without a country to call home. Having to kill a few more souls, whether friend or foe, to earn his independence made no difference to him.

CHAPTER 15

AN UNDERSTANDING

Lacy answered the phone on the first ring, and when she heard Hank's voice, she was both relieved and upset—relieved because he hadn't returned from his meeting with Tate and upset because she thought she should have been there when they met.

"You're right, Lacy," Hank said. "I think Tate is in up to his eyeballs with the drug scene here and maybe statewide as well. But if we're going to find out how this all works, we'll have to be extra careful how we do this or we won't be alive to see this to the end."

Lacy was starting to have regrets about involving him. He hadn't been in Atwood for what seemed a lifetime, and yet she was putting him in harm's way for her own selfish reasons. She knew, however, that there was no chance she could get to the bottom of this situation without him. Perhaps she and Hank could step away by asking the state police for help. But she wasn't sure about the state police, either. Lacy decided that they would, at least for now, keep this investigation to themselves.

"I was at the hospital today, and they brought in another overdose case, but at least he survived," Lacy said as Hank poured a cup of coffee at the kitchen table. They had survived another night in the house together, and he was enjoying every moment of it.

"Did you get a chance to talk to the patient and ask about where he got the drugs?" he asked.

Lacy said she was not allowed to talk to the young man, as he was still in withdrawal. "Let's go back there together tomorrow and see if he has anything to offer," she added.

"Sure, why not?" he said, certain she would go with or without him.

The next day, they entered the hospital through the emergency entrance to avoid the front desk, where they'd be spotted by lots of people. Though it was becoming common knowledge that the two of them were together a lot, it was a little less known that Hank was in fact working with her to put an end to the drug problem in town.

The clerk behind the admittance counter recognized Lacy from the night before. "What can I do for you today, Ms. Anderson?"

"I want to check on Mitch McCabe, the patient from the overdose last night. Can you tell me what room he's in?"

"I'm surprised you've not heard, being a reporter with the *Atwood Herald*. But Mitch McCabe died around two this morning shortly after being transferred from ICU to a room in the main hospital."

"Died? How could that have happened? He was getting along so well at ten last night, just before I left."

Hank tugged her arm and led her out into the sunlight, past the entrance to the hospital, and down the driveway to the front walk, where they sat down on a bench.

"I cannot believe how bad this is getting," Lacy said as a tear rolled down her cheek. She looked very tired.

"For what it's worth, I'm getting really pissed off now and really think there needs to be someone held accountable." He attempted to wipe the tear from her cheek with the handkerchief he kept in his jacket pocket. Lacy pushed his hand away.

"I told you once, Hank, I can take care of myself, so keep your pity for someone that needs it."

"I'm just saying we need to be very cautious from now on. We can't afford to stir up more problems than we can handle," he said and put the handkerchief away.

"Bullshit, Maples. We need to start asking all the hard questions and asking them now before this gets any worse and someone else ends up dead like McCabe."

She was right; they could end up that way.

"So, let me know right now, Hank: are you going to be part of the solution or part of the problem?"

He hadn't wanted Lacy, and for that matter anyone, to know just what he had been doing for the last twenty years since his return from Vietnam. But it seemed that, if he was going to help her get the puzzle solved, she should know what all the pieces looked like.

"Lacy, I'll help. But there are some things you need to know about me that will have bearing on this situation here and across the country as well."

"What are you talking about? Is there something you've failed to mention the last few days?"

"I'm not what or who you think I am."

"What are you talking about, Hank? If there is something I need to know, I expect to hear it, and hear it right now."

"I did not show up here in Atwood just to go to Ralph's funeral. It might sound a bit like a coincidence, but I was on my way here just before he died, and his death worked out to give me the perfect cover."

"Perfect cover? What does that mean?"

"Since my return from Vietnam almost twenty years ago, I've worked for an agency of the US government charged with cleaning up issues that involve any type of crimes against the United States that may involve, or seem to involve, soldiers on the run, mostly deserters here and overseas."

"What the hell are you talking about? And how does all that have anything to do with anything here in Atwood?" Lacy scowled. "Let me see if I understand this shit. Your skinny ass gets drafted not long after a loser high school career, and twenty years later, you come back here as some kind of mystery agent and you expect me to believe you because you say so?"

"Lacy, calm down. Give me a bit of time to help you understand what I am trying to tell you."

"Maples, you already got in my pants, so cut the shit and quit trying to impress me. What agency do you work for?" she asked as she raised her index and middle fingers on both hands and made quotation marks in the air when she said agency.

"I can't tell you, but you have to trust me on this."

"So, you can't tell me exactly what you do and who you do it for, and I'm supposed to just trust you." Again with the air quotation marks! Shit!

Shortly after his undercover assignment in Vietnam, Hank was reassigned to the USAIS in Washington, DC. The United States Army Investigation Service was a covert service tasked with bringing to justice those soldiers who had turned on their country in any number of ways, from simple AWOL to more sophisticated crimes such as desertion and even murder.

Sergeant Maples had worked there for almost twenty years until he retired from active duty. Then he immediately went to work as a civilian investigator for USAIS. There was little he could tell Lacy about what he did because of his security clearance. He would have to keep most of the truth from her, but he needed to tell her just enough to make sure they could work together, as it was becoming clear that he needed her as much as she needed him.

Since Hank's agency was covert, he decided to leave out names and such and clue Lacy in as much as his imagination would allow. He only hoped she had enough faith in what he told her to be the truth.

"So here is what I can share with you, and I want you to listen closely, because what I am about to tell you isn't exactly supposed to be for your ears or others."

CHAPTER 16

HELL BREAKS LOOSE

BIEN HOA, VIETNAM, 1967

Evers watched from his hiding place as a Jeep slowly came over the small hill that ran along a rice paddy in the dump they called Vietnam. His heart started to beat faster as he thought about what was going to happen in the next few minutes and how it would change his life forever.

Soon, he would realize the freedom he'd always wanted but for one reason or another never came his way. Tonight would change all that, and he would enjoy his new life to the max! His men were positioned so the asshole Hong and his pal Maples would be caught in crossfire if things went bad and the swap had to turn into a slaughter. To him, it was as good one way as it was the other. In fact, the more he thought about it, he would actually rather just kill both Hong and Sergeant Maples, take the money they had with them, and keep the thousand pounds of MJ to resell. With his newfound wealth, he'd buy a small house on the beach in Thailand and live there the rest of his life.

Hank got out of the Jeep as Hong eased it to a stop behind a guard post and quickly grabbed the duffle with the cash. As was discussed,

Hank was to have the money and Hong would act as the connection to whoever had the drugs.

Hong got out, put on his night vision goggles, and took a look around in front of the guard post. He thought he could see several men hiding in the undergrowth with weapons but was not sure he saw Evers, who would look much bigger in the night vision goggles than the smaller Vietnamese that worked for him. He knew that Evers would be nearby, though, and would kill Maples with the first shot he had the chance to take.

"So where is this guy supposed to be?" Hank asked as he came around the back of the Jeep, keeping his back to the guard post and keeping his eyes on the lookout for a trap.

"Give me a minute to locate him. I'll get him to hold his ground and come back for you," Hong said as he started to move beyond the last perimeter of the guard post. "I have the exact location on the coordinates map. Don't worry. Everything seems to be on schedule."

Hong slipped away into the dark night illuminated only by the moon and the stars. Hank felt a bit uncomfortable with the situation but realized he had to trust Hong because he had no other choice.

Hank went over to one of the men that was on guard and was controlling the sector that he felt would be where the exchange would be made.

"What are your orders, Corporal, for the protection of the post tonight?" Hank asked a man with the name Lumpy on his name tag.

"Protocol for tonight is password to enter, and if there is none or it's wrong, ask no more questions and let the claymore do the talking," Lumpy said.

Hank let him know that there was a special operation going on and that he knew the password, and so did the other man involved in this operation tonight, thanked him, and told him that in addition to the password he and his other operative would add at the end of the password an extra word—"four." Hank told Lumpy that if things were going well, he was going out beyond the line and to be sure that he followed orders. Lumpy assured Maples that orders would be followed to the letter.

Hong spotted Evers about seventy-five yards down and to the north of the perimeter that the 173rd was guarding, and when Evers saw him, he raised his weapon just to chest high and told Hong to raise his hands. At first, Hong felt panic because he could tell that Evers was not only selling pot, but that his eyes were half closed and red, and the smell of marijuana and whiskey were on his breath.

"What the fuck, Evers? What are you doing all screwed up on this night of all nights?" Hong scolded. He could also sense other eyes on him and thought Evers' men must be watching from the tree line about twenty-five yards from the small clearing they were standing in.

Evers eyed Hong and with a snarl said, "I'm not sure I need you anymore, you shithead gook. I think I can finish off this job without you and keep the entire payoff to myself. Now just put the gun down and let's talk for a minute. Let me make sure you understand what will happen if I don't return to Maples in another five minutes."

Hong tried to explain to Evers that the deal would only go down if he got back to Maples through the guard post and that Maples let him know the exact location of the swap. Hong could tell that Evers was high enough that he wasn't really listening and didn't understand much of what he was trying to tell him, so he decided to make sure that this deal would only go down if he could take charge of the situation and keep Evers from fucking the whole thing up.

Back behind the perimeter, Hank couldn't see Hong, but due to a small transmitter he had placed under Hong's jacket collar when he wasn't looking, he could hear the muted conversation very well. His suspicions about Hong were now vindicated, and he wondered if he could trust Lieutenant Hanger.

Hong had contemplated the life he'd lived to this point and wondered if there was much more of it left. He'd been raised in Ohio by Vietnamese immigrants who came to the US to live a better life than they had in Vietnam, where his father was a nurse and his mother a schoolteacher. They had the opportunity to escape the war-torn country, and they did. As Hong grew older, he began to hate America because of the relentless treatment he was subjected to in his younger years in high school and college. Even though he spoke perfect English and understood American history better than most of his classmates, he was constantly looked down upon as someone who didn't deserve to be a first-class citizen.

When he graduated from college, he decided to return to Vietnam to do what he could to make the USA's effort harder. That's when he became involved with the US Army as a liaison to the command in Saigon. The fact that he had a degree from a college in the US and spoke perfect English made him an excellent choice by the Army to be a liaison between the US Command and the NVA. Little did the Army know that Hong's plan was to seek revenge on the US for the way he had been treated over the last ten years of his life. The only thing he regretted was that his parents would be devastated by the deeds he hoped to accomplish. They were very patriotic to their adoptive country despite being ridiculed and belittled. Hong was about to get even, or was he?

Hong looked Evers in the eye and tried to take charge of the situation. "Listen to me, Evers, and I will only say this once. You have no chance of getting this deal done without me, because I have the password to get back through the outpost and give the info of the whereabouts of the meet up to Maples, who expects me and only me to come back through in the next ten minutes. So either let me do my job and set up Maples for the kill, or just go ahead and kill me now and take your chances without me. I can tell you now you'll never make it out of here alive."

Hong thought he had nothing to lose by taunting Evers and was ready to die here on this spot if he couldn't convince Evers that what he told him was true.

"Okay, Hong. Get your ass back through the perimeter and get Maples and the money out here and do it quickly."

Hong approached the outpost, and when he was challenged for the password, he gave it and was passed through and escorted to the spot where Hank was waiting. Hong had no idea Hank had heard everything and had taken the time to relay the information to Lieutenant Hanger, though he still had doubts about trusting Hangar, since he and Hong seemed to be tight. If Hank was wrong and Hanger and Hong were in this together, he would never make it out of here alive.

CHAPTER 17

MEANS TO AN END

"You want the truth, Lacy? I hope you can handle it. And once you hear what I'm about to tell you, your life will be in danger just as mine is almost every day. So you need to let me know right now whether you want to know what's going on and get involved or maybe be smarter and walk away now."

"Can I hear what you have to tell me and then let you know?" asked Lacy.

"Sorry, but once you know what I'm doing here, you'll be in as much danger as I am. And if you aren't careful, you can end up as dead as me."

Lacy thought for a few minutes. Then, for some reason, she simply said, "I'm in. Let's hear what you have to say, and I'll take my chances."

"So here's the deal. Believe it or not, this all goes back to Ralph and Sheriff Tate. My agency was alerted to a situation that was happening right here in Atwood. You were spot on when you told me that Tate was a murderer. You have no idea just how bad he is. His involvement is not only around here but across the entire half of the United States."

Hank went on to explain in detail how information obtained by USAIS hooked Tate to an unidentified drug dealer that had escaped a trap set in Vietnam many years ago and for some reason found his way to Atwood and the surrounding area. Maybe the rural setting had provided space to operate without much attention.

"I still don't understand what Ralph's death has to do with any of this," Lacy said. "Ralph was just a happy-go-lucky guy with not much ambition other than to have a few beers, tell some jokes, and smoke a joint or two. That hadn't changed much since high school days."

"Do you remember the night the Clancy boy was killed in a car wreck almost twenty years ago?" Lacy nodded. "Ralph was the driver of the car that hit Clancy, and because Ralph had been drinking, he was going to face some serious time in jail because he had some priors. I was with Ralph that night and was pretty drunk as well. Ralph told me to stay in the car. He got out to check on the other driver and came back and said everything was okay, that he was going to drop me off and then get his tow truck, return to the crash site, and tow the driver and his car back to town. We know now that Sheriff Tate helped Ralph avoid jail time by covering up the details of the wreck. Tate was in control of Ralph from that point on."

"And just how do you know all this?" Lacy asked.

"Well, as I said, USAIS has followed clues that have shed light on this old situation because we've been able to track an American deserter to this general area. And in investigating the events from twenty years ago, it seems to suggest that Tate and this drug dealer had some kind of connection and that Ralph had been used a pawn by Tate for years. The information comes from a source, someone we think Ralph must have confided in."

Lacy looked at Maples with a puzzled look in her eye and shared with him. "All this information seems too much to understand all at once. And why would Ralph commit suicide?" she asked.

"Not sure, but he must have somehow known that Tate was feeling the heat of our investigation. Maybe Ralph felt like he'd be caught up in it somehow and be held accountable for the death of the Clancy boy. Or maybe his death wasn't a suicide at all."

"Ralph was murdered?"

"We don't know that, Lacy. But we do know Tate is ruthless. Perhaps Ralph was involved with Tate's operation. Sometimes it is easier to take the path Ralph took rather than step up and be responsible for and take the punishment for your crimes."

Hank told Lacy that if she had any more questions he would let her ask rather than offer any more information. "I know that this must all sound crazy, but the criminal world doesn't play by the same rules as the rest of us."

CHAPTER 18

UNTIL DEATH DO WE PART

BIEN HOA, VIETNAM, 1967

As Hong approached, Hank tried to hide his agitation. He knew he was being double crossed but wasn't sure how it would play out. Evers and Hong were in cahoots, but did they trust each other?

"Did you find the dealer all right?" Hank asked. "Is everything set to go?"

Hank knew he was being set up for the kill and wanted to give Hong a bit of rope with which to hang himself, so when Hong took a moment too long to answer, Hank just took it in stride. Hong gathered all his strength and looked him square in the eye and said, "Yeah, and he has all the dope with him and seems to be alone," Hong lied, not knowing that Maples had heard the entire conversation on the bug he had placed under his collar.

"So let's get the show on the road. Remember to keep your weapon at the ready. As soon as he takes the cash and hands over the marijuana, make sure he stays put, and I'll place him under arrest," Hank said. "If he tries to escape, don't think twice about taking him out, got it?"

"No problem for me, Sergeant," Hong lied. Hank could see the slight twitch in Hong's eye that told him that Hong was about to do something desperate.

Hong could tell that, or at least thought, Maples wasn't trusting him anymore and figured that he would need to do something surprising if he was to get out of this with his life. He'd also love to have some of the cash Maples had with him to use as bait to trap Evers. Maples picked up the bag with the cash and hopped in the Jeep with Hong. They started through the perimeter to meet Evers. Once down the road a ways, Hong, who was in the passenger seat, grabbed the money bag and jumped out of the moving vehicle. Once he hit the ground, he took off as fast as he could, using the hedgerow around a rice paddy for cover. Stunned, Hank slammed on the brakes, threw the shifter in reverse, and headed back to the spot where Hong had fled. He grabbed his M16 and two extra magazines and headed out into the night after Hong and the money. A half moon provided the only light, and he knew that as much as it would help him, it would also be to his harm as they could use the stars and moon to see him.

Hong fled toward the rendezvous spot that he and Evers had agreed to. He paused for a moment to see if he could get a sight line on Hank and eliminate one half of what he considered a dual threat to his life. He knew Hank would kill him on sight, and he'd also lost trust in Evers to kill Maples as they had planned.

Evers watched from a vantage point of slightly higher ground as the drama unfolded. He could see that Hong was running along the edge of rice paddy but wasn't able to see the money bag. He knew, though, that something had gone off plan, and he would have to change plans in the middle of what was turning out to be a cluster fuck if there ever was one.

Hong knew that if Evers was watching all this, he would take a different look at shooting Maples and taking the money and giving him the marijuana. Hong was going to have to play one side against the other if he had any chance of getting out of this jam.

From his hiding place, Hong spotted Maples and watched as he got closer and closer to the area that Evers was supposed to meet up with Maples and Hong. The shit was about to hit the fan, because it wouldn't take Evers long to find out that Maples no longer had the cash that was to be paid to Evers. Hong thought for a few minutes that seemed like hours and came up with a plan to have his cake and eat it too, as the old saying went. He would bury the money and return to base camp. Then, when the opportunity came up, he would come back and get the money. The chance of Maples living much longer in this darkness wasn't good, and he also knew now that Evers would kill him right after he killed Maples.

Evers watched as things unfolded below the hill he was watching from. He could see now that Hong was burying something, and as he looked over at the side where Maples was approaching from, he could tell that he wasn't carrying anything large enough to be a money bag with that much money in it. He guessed that Hong had double crossed Maples and now was attempting to cheat him out of the money as well. Evers thought that killing Hong would be easier now that he knew Hong was not only a traitor but a thief as well.

Hong took out a piece of paper and made a small map where he had buried the money then started back to base camp. As soon as he stood, Evers took aim and fired off two rounds at Hong's back. Fortunately for Hong, because of the darkness of the night, both rounds missed their marks.

Seeing the muzzle flash, Maples rushed forward to the spot where he'd last seen it. His combat training failed him as he got anxious and closed too quickly on whoever had fired at Hong. Evers fired off three quick rounds at the approaching Maples and could plainly see that at least one of them found its target.

Pain like Maples had never felt before was coming from his right shoulder area, and he could feel the blood running down the front of his field jacket. He could barely feel anything at all on the right side of his body and had no idea where his M16 was. After a few minutes, he located it and threw it in the Jeep. He wasn't sure he would be able to fire it anyway, with his wound, but thought he would rather have it and not need it than need it and not have it. He decided to try to head for base camp. He would hopefully live to fight another day.

As fortunate as it was for Hong not getting hit by Evers' shots, it was just as unfortunate that he had jumped out of the Jeep before Maples had told him about the change in password. His plan was to get back to camp and report Maples dead and wait until the next day or so to return for the money.

Private Lumpy and the rest of the guards were on high alert when the shooting beyond the perimeter started. Even though the number of shots fired were few, they had been trained that until someone up the chain of command gave the order to stand down, protocol needed to be followed to the absolute letter. Hong approached the line, and as Lumpy heard footsteps, he challenged the small-figured man approaching his checkpoint. Remembering what Maples told him, Lumpy challenged a second time. Following orders when the password was answered once again incorrectly, Private Lumpy had no choice but to push the trigger to the blasting cap attached to the claymore mines that protected the perimeter. When dawn broke, a patrol advanced beyond the line, and they found what was left of Duon Hong. It wasn't much.

Maples heard the Claymore and wondered if Hong had tried to get back to base camp and make up a lie about what happened that night. Evers was about to rush Maples and finish the job when he decided that killing him could wait, since he would now have the time to go get the cash that Hong buried, keep the marijuana, and find another buyer. Since Maples heard no more gunshots, he headed to the Jeep and, as quickly as he could, dragged himself into the driver's seat. Though he was in great pain, he got it started and headed in the direction of base camp, though he erred on the side of caution and drove with the lights off.

Evers came off the hill, signaled to the rest of his men to follow him, and led them to the spot where he had seen Hong bury the money. The four men Evers had with him started to dig up the money and were laughing and having a good time doing so. As usual, Evers had given all the men pot to smoke. They were giddy and relaxed, just as Evers had hoped.

When the four men turned around to show Evers they had all the money, there was no fear showing in their eyes as Evers simply said, "Goodbye, gooks," and emptied the remaining rounds in his clip into their small bodies, effectively leaving no witness to the night's events other than Sergeant Hank Maples. And one way or another, Maples would die, just like the rest of the evening's participants. Evers now had the one thousand pounds of marijuana and forty thousand more US dollars to add to the two hundred thousand he had in his stash. Time to get out of there and find that new life he had been craving for a long time.

CHAPTER 19

NOT SO SAFE

Tate saw the name on his cell phone screen and was in no mood to have a pointless discussion with the man pulling the strings—*his strings*. Bad enough that the man was now calling him almost weekly if not more. Hank Maples and that bitch Lacy Anderson were making his job harder than it had been in years.

Tate had been able to make a wealthy future for himself, and he wasn't about to let a local newspaper reporter and Vietnam vet screw that up. He'd been smart about his ill-gotten gains. He stashed the money, not flaunting it or buying lavish things a small-time sheriff couldn't possibly afford. Soon he would have enough hidden cash that he could leave this pitiful place and live elsewhere in luxury for the rest of his life. And who knew? He might just take Claire with him. Or maybe he would find someone even better.

Tate exhaled and took the call.

"Tate, this is your last chance to get rid of our problem. Maples is getting too close to finding out what we are doing, and if he does, we're in deep shit. If that happens, you'll be the first one to get a bullet in the head, and you'll never see it coming."

"Fuck you!" Tate yelled. "You need to think about who you are talking to, you fuckhead. Just because you hide behind that crazy son of a bitch you brought over here doesn't mean you can't be touched as well. I am doing what needs to be done, and when the time is right, Maples will die and this shitty mess will be over and you will get your goddamn money and then some if it all works out. I might as well give you that bitch Lacy Anderson as well. Maybe you can have some fun with her before she dies. Now back off my ass and let me do what you're paying me to do."

Before Tate could hang up, he heard the phone on the other end click off. He wondered if he'd been too far out of line. He guessed he would find out.

Lacy woke up early and reached over to the other side of the bed, patting around in search of Hank. When she realized he wasn't there, she quickly picked up her night shirt that had been casually tossed on the floor in the heat of the night and went into the kitchen where she could smell coffee. She spotted Hank out on the front porch, slowly sipping on a cup of the newly brewed coffee. She poured herself a cup and went out the door, quietly sitting in a chair opposite him. He glanced over in her direction and smiled.

"Morning, Lacy," he greeted.

Lacy looked at Hank and thought to herself that this situation with Hank was starting to get a little too comfortable. "Morning yourself. How long have you been up? And thanks for the pot of coffee."

"Been up most of the night. I got a call from HQ around midnight with some interesting news about what might be happening around here. Seems likely that a man I was hunting for in Vietnam may be in the country now, and if so, he's likely to be looking for me to kill me for what happened many years ago. If that happens to be true, it might explain why the drug activity is on the upswing here."

Lacy looked concerned and puzzled at the same time and asked Hank what he could tell her. She knew from previous conversations that he would only tell her information that wasn't classified, but she also wondered what danger she might be in if her story exposed dangerous people.

"Listen, Hank, I realize that there are things you can't tell me. If you don't feel you can trust me, we should go our separate ways. If we cross paths again, good, but if not, too bad for both of us. I think you like this situation between us as much as I do."

With that being said, Lacy started to get up. As she did so, Hank grabbed her by the hand and pulled her back down in the seat, stared into her bright eyes, and leaned over and kissed her.

"Okay, Lacy. I'm going to tell you more than I should. But you need to know that once you commit to listening, there is no turning back. The man you are about to hear about is one badass criminal who has no fear for his life and none for the life of anyone else who gets in his way. I can say that from past experiences with him."

CHAPTER 20

THE KILLING ZONE

BIEN HOA, VIETNAM, 1967

Maples wasn't sure if he heard the shots fired first or out of the corner of his eye saw movement to his left about fifty yards out. He could tell that the gunfire was not trained on him, and he was quick, though still in pain, to turn the Jeep around and head into the area just up the dirt path. He knew he should return to base camp for medical treatment for his wounds, but he also thought that he had a chance to capture whoever did this. He assumed it must be the man they called Evers, who would be long gone by the morning light.

The pain was lessening now, probably just getting numb, but the blood was still oozing from the wound in his shoulder, so as bad as he wanted to rush to the sight of the muzzle flashes, he put the Jeep in neutral and put on the emergency brake. Hank took out his knife and cut some strips of cloth from a jacket he'd tossed on the seat beside him, making a tourniquet out of them. Getting it on with one good arm proved not so easy, but after a few precious minutes, he got it on and could see, though it was very dark, that the blood was starting to stop. He hit the gas and drove ahead as fast as he could without lights on.

Rains had made the trails very muddy, and Sergeant Maples put the transmission into four-wheel drive, since the trail was now heading almost straight up.

Evers was on the run and hated the fact that he wasn't only seemingly having to leave this great money-making gig behind but was, after all these years, about to be caught. He knew drastic measures needed to be taken to avoid what would be his capture and, for his crimes, the death penalty. If he had to kill another and it happened to be an American, so be it! *Better him than me*, he thought. He stopped running up the hill and decided to ambush Maples and put an end to this shit tonight.

Maples was blinded by the pain in his shoulder but decided that he had to finish what he started now. As close as he was, he may never get another chance like this. Evers could hear a Jeep coming up the hill but decided that he would make his stand here and take his chances with how this night ended up.

As Maples was rounding a big turn in the trail, the Jeep sputtered and the engine coughed a few times and quit running. A glance at the gas gauge told a disappointed Maples all he needed to know. His shoulder blazing in pain, he realized that he had come too far to go back, even if he had fuel to do so. He would push on, though now on foot. It didn't escape Hank that now the advantage he may have had over Evers with the Jeep was now gone and he would be on equal footing with the man he was after.

Evers watched from above and smiled when Maples left the safety of the Jeep. He now thought that because he had the advantage of higher ground, he would prevail. He watched Maples get out of the Jeep and go around to the back of it. Though it was very dark except for the moon, he watched Maples take out the M16 and several magazines.

Evers grabbed an AK47 and ammo from one of the Vietnamese he had killed when they dug up the money that Hong had buried, and he had at least two hundred rounds with him. For someone as strong as he was, the weight was of no concern. He got off the trail and got into a rice paddy on the right side of the trail so when Sergeant Maples got in range, he would usher him into the next world. Having qualified as an expert in marksmanship in basic training, Evers knew he could kill Maples from at least seventy-five yards but wanted to see the look in his eyes when he knew he was going to die, so he marked out a killing zone of about ten yards, taking a chance that Maples would see him first. *Not very likely,* he thought.

Hank saw, or thought he saw, movement to his left. After pausing for a few moments, he started out again, only to feel the same sensation to his right. He stopped to listen, and as he did, he was confronted by four Vietnamese. His life flashed before his eyes as he thought of all the things in his future that would never come to pass. Though never religious, he said a quick prayer and expected to die right there. He was quickly wrestled to the ground and held there by two of the men. He looked up at the apparent leader. The man motioned for Hank to stay silent by placing a finger to his lips.

Up on the hill, Evers could hear nothing nor could he see anything happening below. In fact, he wondered if Sergeant Maples had died from his wound. He could only hope so.

Below, the leader of the small group with Maples said in very broken English that they wanted to help kill "Drug Man," who they watched kill four of their comrades. The man said Hank would be released when they finished their mission of revenge. As they crept up the hill, they had no idea where Evers was, but they were sure he was in the area, and if the Cong were good at anything, it was just this type of warfare.

As good as they thought they were, they weren't good enough. The first burst from Evers' AK47 took out the first two Vietnamese. The last two started to run down the hill as fast as they could but stopped when they heard no return firing.

Hank could only fire with one arm and released the first clip in his M16 toward the flash point of the AK47. For some reason, there was no return fire from Evers, and at first, Maples thought he might have been lucky. He waited for what seemed like minutes but in reality was only a few seconds. He had learned early on that the longer one waited, the unluckier one got, and when he motioned for the last two Vietnamese to follow him, to their credit, they charged ahead, following Maples the last fifty yards up the hill.

Evers knew instantly that he was out of luck, and if the chopper he was waiting for was even ten seconds late, he might never need another ride again.

Hank and his unlikely comrades spotted a lone figure almost at the top of the hill, and at the same time, they opened fire with all that they had. Just as they were closing on Evers, the unmistakable sound of an Army Huey came from above. Hank and his two companions watched in shock as the chopper made a circle and started to approach Evers' position. He was surprised and more than that was shocked when he saw Evers run for the open door. In an instant, less than the time it took to blink an eye, Hank realized that help was indeed on the way, but not for who he had hoped. As much as he hated to do it, he and the men with him opened fire on the chopper and on Evers as well, who was sprinting for the open door. As Evers got closer to the chopper, Hank ran to get as close as he could to try to grab Evers as he was about to jump onboard. He fired what was left in his magazine, flipped it over, slammed it into the M16, and fired the entire clip in a few seconds. He could tell from the screams, and he was close enough to see, that the bottom part of Evers' leg was awash in blood and that from the knee down, there was very little left. As the Huey lifted off, Hank tried to catch a glimpse of the pilot. He thought the fatigue he felt was about to take over, and he had a hard time believing who he thought he saw in the seat at the controls. *What the fuck!*

Lieutenant Hanger had an almost wicked look in his eye as he veered the chopper up and headed south from the top of the hill. Sergeant Maples was sure that Evers would bleed out and die before he could reach the medical help he was going to need. Maples opened a small notebook and entered the time and place Evers was killed.

💀

Hanger put the chopper down and quickly put a tourniquet around Evers' leg. It was clear that the leg would have to go.

"What took you so goddamn long to get here, you fucker?" Evers moaned. "I need to get somewhere to fix this leg."

Hanger thought that if he had all the money they worked so hard for and the drugs with him, he would simply put a round in Evers' head and head back to base camp. But he needed Evers to take him to the stash.

"I am going to take you to Vung Tau to the field hospital. We should be there in five minutes. I will tell them that you're an undercover operative, and they'll take care of you. Then we'll get you out of there. That leg might have to go, but with all the money we have, once we get back to the States, we can get you somewhere and get you fitted for a prosthesis." Hanger had foreseen this exact circumstance and had prepared a fake set of papers that would identify Evers as an undercover agent rather than the criminal he was.

CHAPTER 21

NO TURNING BACK

Lacy sat up with an alertness in her eyes that Hank hadn't seen before.

"So here's what's happening, and here's how this situation came to be," Hank said. "Several years ago, in Vietnam, I was in charge of tracking down a nasty drug dealer and deserter named Ronald Evers. He had deserted his post and for a long time was dealing drugs with a bunch of Viet Cong in the jungles of the country.

"On many occasions, there would be a firefight with American infantry, and on more than one occasion, there weren't only enemy wounded and killed but several times American soldiers were killed as well," Hank said.

Lacy sat mesmerized by the story. "So what does that have to do with anything happening here?" she asked, and as she did, she sat a bit closer to Hank and put her hand on his shoulder to calm him down a bit. She could see he was getting a bit on edge as he related the story to her. Hank felt her soft touch, and he could sense Lacy was trying to comfort him. He suddenly felt more at ease.

"Evers found out that I was on his trail and was getting close to ending his operation. I was within a few yards of him when the shit the fan, and I was shot in my approach to him and his small gang of

Viet Cong. There was a short firefight after I was hit, but I managed to shoot him back. I thought that I was going to finally catch him, but just as I came up the last hill, a chopper swooped in and started to fire on my position." Hank explained to Lacy that at first he thought that the chopper, which had 1st Cav marking, was coming to help him out but was quick to find out that the opposite was true. "Not only that, but at the controls of the Huey was the leader of our task force, a Lieutenant Hanger, who was obviously not the person I thought he was." Hank went on to tell Lacy that no one could make any sense of the relationship between Hanger and Evers, but however they got together, it was proving to be a daunting task to deal with.

"I was hit in the shoulder and arm and was taken to the hospital. I was there for ten days getting patched up and was hoping to get back to my unit and continue the hunt for Evers and Hanger. Unfortunately, that wasn't going to happen, as the hospital commander was very clear to my CO that he was writing orders that would rotate me back to the States. So ended my hunt for Evers."

"So are you saying that Hanger and Evers are in this area? And if so, what are they doing here? How does any of that have to do with what's going on here with drugs and shootings? Are you saying that the shots fired at my house had something to do with them?"

"I think so," said Hank, "but I can't prove it yet, and my agency has lost track of both. There are reports that Evers is still missing and may be dead, but no word on Hanger. There is some talk that one of Evers' men is the one here in the country doing the drugs and maybe even looking to settle the score with me for almost killing Evers. In fact, I might have if he didn't get medical help quickly after the firefight."

Lacy was starting to shiver a bit, and Hank could see the fear in her eyes. He had no good way to calm her down, so he continued with the facts as he knew them. "Reports from USAIS are conflicted, though, and some think that Hanger and Evers made it back to the States. There was also the issue of the missing money and lots of drugs as well. If they ended up getting all that out of the country, they would be wealthy men and could cause a lot of trouble with that kind of cash. They could easily find their way back to the States, though they'd have to do so in a roundabout way."

Lacy was visibly shaken, and as tough as she thought she was, she had begun to wonder how she could be in the middle of such a mess and if she was indeed up to the task of sticking it out to the end.

"Why here? Why would they pick this area and Atwood in particular to set up a drug operation? This is basically in the middle of nowhere, Hank."

Hank had already told her more than he thought he should have but decided that she could be in more danger if he left out any information that she should know to keep her as safe as could be. After all, not having full knowledge could be as dangerous as not enough. "USAIS has come to understand that Evers and Hanger somehow are connected to several unknowns in this general area, that they have set up an operation here hoping to avoid any major cities and blend into the community."

CHAPTER 22

CHARLES HANGER

VIETNAM, 1967

Lieutenant Hanger looked at Evers in the chopper seat next to him and thought, *What a piece of shit.* Six months earlier, after his reprimand, he had met Evers in a backwoods bar and started what had turned out to be a relationship that was both regretful and rewarding at the same time because of the money he was making outside the laws of the Army. Hanger knew he would quit the Army at the end of this current tour, which was in another six months.

He only had to cover up his actions until then. Now, though, because he was sure Maples saw him, there was no return to base camp, and with a stolen Huey to boot. If he could get deep enough in the jungle, he might even be able to keep the chopper. He needed to be in and out of the hospital ASAP. Hanger had a look of disgust on his face as he considered what he had become and how it all had started out for him. As he flew the chopper south to the evacuation hospital that he needed to get Evers to, he couldn't stop thinking about how he'd gotten to this point.

From junior high school on, it was plain to see that everyone expected Charles Hanger to not only do well in school but in life. By his senior year in high school, he was Mister Everything, captain of the football team, which won the state championship with him as the quarterback. Upon graduation from high school, he was given an appointment to West Point. Once again, he was a natural leader of other cadets and quarterbacked the Army football team to a respectful ten and six record and graduated with full honors. He went to flight school at Fort Rucker, Alabama, to learn to fly choppers. After graduating, once again at the top of his class, he was assigned to the 1st Cavalry Division, flying troops into and out of landing zones in the rice paddies.

Then the shit hit the fan! Word came from Charlie Company's Fourth Platoon that they had six men stranded and needed evacuation from a hot LZ just a few miles up the An Khe pass. Hanger ran to his Huey and fired it up without orders to do so and in fact was radioed that he needed to abort his effort due to weather conditions and that the six trapped troops would need to hold off the Viet Cong another five minutes when the monsoon was due to pass. Hanger had heard the message on the radio, but as was his nature, he ignored the chain of command and went to try to rescue the stranded troops.

As he approached the coordinates sent by the trapped squad, he could see them with his night vision equipment and radioed to them to move to the rear of the field they were in. He watched as four of the troops carried the remaining two on their shoulders and proceeded to do what Hanger had suggested. Under heavy fire and pounding rain from the monsoon, Hanger lowered the Huey to the clearing, and the squad quickly ran for the open doors of the chopper. Hanger moved to the opposite side where the forty-caliber door gun was and laid ground fire until the troops were in the back of the chopper. Hanger had left base camp so quickly and without orders he didn't have time to round up his usual door gunner, and even if he could have, he wouldn't have done so to keep the gunner out of trouble if things went wrong. Once all were aboard, he let one of the men from the trapped squad man the door gun and went back to the controls of the chopper. Through heavy fire from the Viet Cong, he managed to get off the ground and head to base camp with all the troops safely aboard.

When he arrived at base camp, the chopper was met by medics and Jeeps that took the wounded to the hospital. Also on scene was his commanding officer with a grim look on his face. The Huey had sustained a good bit of damage, and though he had no idea, Hanger himself was about to get damaged as well. Colonel Collins grabbed Hanger by the arm and got in his face.

"Who the fuck do you think you are to not obey orders?" the Colonel asked.

Thinking that the Colonel should be congratulating him for a job well done, Hanger lost control and took a swing at the Colonel. It landed square on his superior's jaw and dropped him to the ground. Several men around them quickly separated the two men, but as the Colonel got up, Hanger hit him again. It took even more men to pull Hanger off the Colonel, who was wiping a bit of blood from his face.

Collins looked at Hanger and told him that while he admired his courage displayed tonight, he was indeed going to make it difficult for Hanger to ever get promoted again. And as long as Hanger was under his command, he would never fly again. Hanger made up his mind that from that point on, he would be all about himself. *Fuck the Army.*

So here he was hooked up to some low-life deserter, drug dealer, and as disgusted as he was about the piece of shit he was trying to save, he knew that he himself was not much better, and in fact, because of his background, he might even be worse. He had to be sure to save this fuckhead, Evers, so he could lead Hanger back to the money they'd stashed and the drugs as well. But staying on task, he landed the Huey at the Army field hospital, and with the fake papers in hand, he helped Evers to the emergency entrance to the tent-like war zone hospital. Medics that picked up Evers were grim in their opinion of the leg and rushed him back to surgery as soon as Hanger showed them the fake papers that made Evers look to be an undercover hero. *What a bunch of shit*, Hanger thought. He'd explained that whatever the result, Evers would need to be back on the chopper in the morning.

The medics carried Evers back to the operating room, and Hanger was led to a makeshift waiting room that consisted of a few odd chairs and a couch that could serve as a bed if someone needed to catch a few hours of sleep while they waited. Just as Hanger was about to doze off, a doctor wearing a surgical gown and mask approached.

"I am Colonel Holding with First Med Surge here. I'll be working with the man you brought in." Hanger stood and started to salute, but the doctor waved him off. "Here we are all just workers, and rank doesn't mean a thing to most of us." He sat beside Hanger. "I understand that Sergeant Adams is an undercover MP, is that correct?" Holding asked.

Hanger had handed the medics the fake paperwork that gave Evers a new identification. "Yes sir, and we need him fixed and ready to get back to base camp for a debriefing right away," he said.

The doctor took a deep breath. "That's not going to be possible, Lieutenant, because they are sedating Adams now because I'm going to have to remove what is left of the leg. Then Adams will need to be here for at least three days before he can be moved."

"You don't understand, Doctor. We are about to close down a situation that has cost many people their lives, including some of our own troops, and he needs to be in An Khe tomorrow so the brass can proceed." Holding stood and without another word and left for the operating room. Hanger watched the doctor walk away and thought, *Colonel, you have no idea!*

Five hours later, Hanger, now asleep on the couch, felt a tap on his shoulder. When he looked up through exhausted eyes, he could see it was Dr. Holding.

"Your man did great, Lieutenant. We've moved him to a bed in ward three, which is in the back of the hospital. He is under heavy sedation, but he wants to see you ASAP. I think he must be made of steel, because he seems very alert and says he isn't feeling much pain. I have cleared it with the ward supervisor, so go on back."

Hanger walked toward the back of the hospital and was sure that somehow Evers had some hidden drugs on him that was getting him through the pain. Hanger pushed back the curtain, shielding Evers from the rest of the ward. When he looked in Evers' eyes, he could see a burning hate unlike any he'd ever seen before. "Glad to see you made it through the surgery," Hanger said.

Evers, in a weak voice, responded, "Fuck you. If you hadn't been late, I would still have two legs and we could be out of this fucking stinking country by now."

"Calm down, Evers. We'll still get out, just not quite so soon," Hanger said. "Don't forget we still have the chopper, and it's being refueled as we speak, but you need to get some rest."

"Bullshit. We need to get out first thing in the morning. How long do you think it will take for your outfit to realize you aren't coming back? And with their chopper to boot. And another thing, I need to find that fucker Maples and kill that son of a bitch for what he did to my leg. I may never walk on my own two legs again, but that prick will never walk again at all when I am done with him."

CHAPTER 23

THREATS AND CONSEQUENCES

The round exploded just over his head as it came through the back window of Tate's car. As he stepped down on the accelerator, he watched as the speedometer climbed to eighty, ninety, and then almost one hundred miles an hour as he started to put some distance between his car and the one following him. Suddenly, another car was coming the opposite way and on his side of the road.

"What the fuck!" he exclaimed. Toughened by life itself and his years on the job, he thought he could handle anything that came his way. But maybe not. He decided to head faster at the oncoming car and hoped he had more balls than the oncoming driver. It was a deadly game of chicken.

The car behind him was gaining as another bullet came in through the shattered back window and exploded the front window. Tate could hardly see the road. He thought he had only two choices, neither of which were good. He could slam on the brakes and hope the car in the back slowed fast enough to avoid a rear-end collision or he could try to swerve out to his left to avoid the car in front. Just as he was making up his mind, his engine exploded and caught fire, most likely from a bullet, and Tate had no choice but to jump out or be burned alive. The car was fully engulfed in flames, and they would soon get to the gas tank in the rear and blow the car the rest of the way up.

The car in the back had come to a stop and just sat there. Tate grabbed his rifle that hung in its holder on the dash and rolled out of the burning car. He hit the ground on his back with the rifle at the ready and then rolled over a few times to the safety of the ditch from which he could hopefully get off a few rounds of his own before they overpowered him and did what they had to do.

Tate was shocked when the light on the car in front flicked on and off several times, as if to taunt him, and started to back up. It then spun around and took off, as did the car in the rear. Tate couldn't believe what had just happened, and it took a full five minutes for his heart to slow to a point that allowed him to breathe a normal breath. Again, he thought to himself, *What the fuck just happened?* Luckily, he had his cell phone with him, and he called the deputy on duty to let him know that he would need a ride back to town and to send a wrecker as well.

Deputy Bronson arrived in about twenty-five minutes, the wrecker following him. When Bronson saw what was left of the sheriff's car, all he could do was wonder out loud what had happened. "Who did you piss off?" he asked as he put his sidearm back in his holster. He had come prepared to defend his boss. If he had any idea how crooked Tate was, he showed no sign of it.

Tate looked up at Bronson and smiled a curious smile that Bronson confused with intelligence. By the time they got the ruined cruiser on the tow truck, Tate thought he knew what just happened, and though he could tell no one what he was thinking, he decided that he'd had enough bullshit from the "Man."

Tate had a few cuts and his hip was sore, but he decided not to go to the hospital. Instead, his deputy drove him home. As soon as Tate grabbed a cold beer from the bar fridge and sat down, his phone lit up. He saw on the screen who was calling. As much as he didn't want to answer, he felt that he would be worse off if he didn't.

"So how was your little drive tonight, Sheriff?" Tate started to mutter something, and before he could, the man said, "Tonight was just a little warning, unless you get rid of our little problem, and soon. The next time you decide to take a little drive, you won't come back. Your time is about up, and there is only one outcome that will be acceptable. Maples has to die and soon. He is getting too close, and that is not good. Do you understand?"

Tate saw no way out of the shit he had brought upon himself. All he could offer was a short, "Yes." He had no other choice than to go after Maples. He needed help, and he knew just who would love to do the dirty work that needed to be done.

CHAPTER 24

KING OF THE JUNGLE

VIETNAM, 1967

Hanger could not convince Dr. Holding that it was vital he release Evers to him so the two of them could get back to base camp ASAP, and when Holding told him it would be more like five days before Evers could be moved safely, Hanger came up with a plan that would get him and Evers out of harm's way. Hanger knew that Colonel Collins in An Khe would stop at nothing to get him back and put him in the makeshift jail until he could court marshal him, get him out of the Army altogether—if not worse—and have him sentenced to prison. Hanger decided he needed to get Evers out of the hospital during the day rather than the night because chopper traffic was higher in the daytime. His plan was to offer his service to the hospital on the next evacuation run but would instead get Evers from the ward and escape with him into the jungle. The only problem was that, though he could get the chopper up and out, he wasn't sure where he could get to and be safe. But getting out was the first priority.

On day two, Hanger went to Evers to let him know what was about to happen. "You have any idea what you are going to do now to get us out of here?" Evers asked.

"The chopper is up and ready to go whenever you think you have the strength."

"You piece of shit. This is all on me now, and I'll tell you when and where we go from here."

"What is the true range of the Huey?" Evers asked. Hanger told him that at about 127 MPH, they could cover about 330 miles until they ran out of fuel.

"That should be perfect to get to the Refuge."

"What is the Refuge?" Hanger asked and was dumbfounded when Evers explained that there was an entire outpost of disgruntled American troops that were all AWOL from their units and were working the back jungles in support of those like him that were at odds with the war and the politics behind it. The Refuge was just over the Cambodian border and basically off the grid of the US Command.

"If you can get me there, I will be taken care of by the doctors that have decided that this isn't the war that some in the US think it is. There are also a big contingent of Vietnamese that are against the war as well, and everyone there works hard to support those that have like values. Some call them traitors; some call them patriot. I know that you're West Point, and I am just a shit off the streets, but you have to remember it's the politicians that make all the enemies across the world pretty much for their own greed and then put guys like us in to do the dirty work. Thousands are killed in the name of freedom, but in the end, the losers are just as free as the winners, just a little bit poorer. And in the meantime, the very families that are told their loved ones died fighting a common enemy have trouble surviving in the world that was just saved for them to enjoy. Give me a fucking break."

Two hours later, Hanger had the refueled Huey up and running and ready to go as soon as he could get Evers out of the ICU. Hanger entered the ward and approached the charge nurse with a request to visit with Evers.

"Sorry, sir, but the orders I have do not allow for a visit from anyone other than the patient's doctors."

Hanger had it up to his ass with protocol. He pulled his sidearm out and pointed it at the nurse's head. "Does this override your orders?"

The nurse looked around for some help, but at this time of night, there was none to be found. With a very shaky voice, she asked what he wanted. "Go get patient Adams and get him ready to go." The charge nurse complied, and within three minutes, Evers was in the hall and ready to go.

With the chopper running and time wasting, Hanger kept the gun pointed at the nurse as she helped Evers out the door of the hospital, carrying a bag of meds.

"Hurry up, you bitch. We need to be on our way," Hanger said as he opened the sliding chopper door and gave Evers a hand up. It was a desolate night out, and it was about to pour rain as Hanger got Evers strapped in and took the bag from the nurse.

Hanger feared the nurse would alert security as soon as they lifted off, so as Hanger powered up the Huey, he pointed the gun at the nurse. He motioned for her to get in the back with Evers, and as frightened as she was, she didn't hesitate to comply. She figured they needed her to help with the patient if something went wrong. She was wrong!

With little less than a gleam of his eye, Evers knew what the signal from Hanger meant. About ten minutes into the flight, Evers, even in his weakened condition and perhaps encouraged by the drugs in his system, grabbed the nurse and, at about one thousand feet in the air, pushed her out the door of the Huey. They would have their head start on anyone that might figure things out and with one less person to worry about.

"So tell me about this place you call the Refuge. I'll need to know exactly where it is so I can make sure we take the shortest route, as we won't have any chance to refuel."

Hanger fed data into the onboard computer that would let him know if they could make it to the place Evers called the Refuge. Evers slipped on the headphones so he could help direct Hanger to the safe ground of the hidden enclave.

"There are hundreds and hundreds of people like me, and now you, where we're going. Just head west to the Cambodian border. It's about fifteen miles into the jungle south and west of Phnom Penh. You will not be able to see it until you are almost on top of it because of the dense overgrowth."

Hanger watched Evers take out a small bottle of whiskey he had somehow managed to acquire and swallow a few pills. Evers quickly dozed off. Hanger knew that he must be getting close, as the needle of the fuel gauge was getting close to empty. Not wanting to make any mistakes, he reached over and shook Evers awake.

"So, where to now?" Hanger asked as he pointed to the bustling city to the north and told Evers that he thought it was Phnom Penh.

"I can't go too close to the outskirts of the city because I'm sure the marking on this chopper identifies us as US, and though Cambodia is not officially in the war, they would love to shoot this Huey down."

Evers blinked as he came awake, and it took him a few seconds to realize just where they were. "Great, must have been out for a good while. It looks like you got us where we need to be." He pointed to a small clearing about two miles to the southwest. "Head for that clearing over there and make three circles above it. Then land on top of that hillside."

"You better be sure, because we're all but empty, and once down, we won't have the ability to get off the ground again." As the chopper bounced and settled on the ground, Hanger asked, "What's gonna happen to all that money and drugs we left behind?"

"Quit worrying. My guys have already recovered it. It's all here waiting for us."

CHAPTER 25

THE MAN FOR THE JOB

Sheriff Tate was irritated and sick of being pushed around. Besides the threats, the only information "the man" gave was a name—Kent Richards—and a phone number. Tate tried the number and was dumped into an answering machine. "Leave no message. I will call you back on another line," the voice that must have been Richards's said in almost a commanding way.

About twenty minutes later, Tate's phone vibrated, and when he looked at the screen, he didn't recognize the number and thought it must have been the call he was waiting for. He answered only using his last name.

"Sheriff Tate, this is Kent Richards. Listen closely and say nothing until I ask you. We need to meet and have a talk in a place that we can be sure no one else will be able to see or hear. And never use my name again. The next phone call will be from a different number."

Tate suggested Smoke Mountain Road, which was the last turn to the right on the state highway at the east end of Atwood. It dead ended into the lake, there was only one way in and out, and you would have to have an off-road vehicle to get through the rugged overgrowth that almost completely covered the old county road. Tate knew that it was never used anymore except in deer season and only then by the heartiest hunters willing to mess up any paint on the truck they used to get there. "I'll find it," Richards said, "and I'll call you when I get there. You will have ten minutes to show up. Don't waste your time getting there before me. I'll have eyes on you from this point on." The line went dead.

Eyes on me? What the fuck is that supposed to mean? Tate thought, but at the same time, he knew that as much as he hated the spot he was in, he valued his life more, and he would do just as he was told, at least for now. He thought how great it would be to finally be rid of that pest Hank Maples and, maybe, the *Atwood Herald* reporter. Maybe he would even settle the score with the man himself. First, though, he would have to figure out a way to cope with the man called Richards. He needed to make sure that Richards thought he was calling all the shots. Tate would have to remain calm until such time that he could take back the control that he deserved.

Richards pulled off the highway onto Smoke Mountain Road and continued to the edge of the lake. He stayed in his truck and dialed his partner's phone to find out just where Tate was. When he heard Tate was still in the sheriff's office, he was relieved. Tate had taken his warning seriously. Richards felt in control and confident. He would have Hank Maples eliminated, and then Sheriff Tate.

Tate looked at the screen on his phone as it vibrated. "Tate, you have ten minutes to get here," Richards said on the other end of the line, "and remember I have eyes on you, so be sure to come alone and make sure you are not followed." The line went dead before he could say another word.

Tate spotted a truck at the end of the gravel lane leading to the lake. He pulled to within ten yards and stopped. Out of the truck stepped a man about six foot three with a very athletic build and hair down to the back of his neck. Tate got out of his car and began to approach the man, who raised a shotgun and leveled it at him.

"Far enough," the man said and waved the shotgun, indicating for Tate to move to his left toward an overgrown oak tree. "Come over here and sit on the ground."

I'm being treated like the enemy. This shit is getting deep, Tate thought.

The man had given Tate the money to give to Richards to kill Maples. As Richards approached Tate's position, he spoke in very abrupt tones. "Money?" Richards asked. Without getting up, Tate asked if he could reach into his jacket pocket. Richards nodded approval and added, "Very slowly."

Tate did as asked and handed the envelope to Richards. "It's all there, thirty-five thousand, to make sure you do this and fast. There is lots of pressure to have this over with, and if you have to kill the bitch as well, there will be ten grand more," Tate said.

For a moment, he thought he was back in charge until Richards kicked him in the stomach, stepped back, and waved a gun in Tate's face. "And for another ten grand, I might just kill you as well."

Sheepishly, Tate looked at Richards and tried to smile over his fear. "No need for that, Richards. We are all in this together."

Richards sneered, and his face contorted into what Tate felt was pure evil. With just a flick of his wrist, Richards put the envelopes in his pocket and kicked Tate again, this time in the head. The last thing Tate heard before he passed out was Richards laughing as he slammed the door to the truck and sped off.

When Tate awoke, it was just getting dark, and he had a pounding headache. He stumbled to his car and opened the glove box. He removed a bottle of Jack Daniels, took a healthy swig and then another as he sat back in the car seat. He closed his eyes and thanked God he was still alive, though he had no idea for how much longer.

CHAPTER 26

INSIDE THE REFUGE

CAMBODIA, 1967

Hanger landed the Huey and shut the engine down. As he did so, he looked at the fuel gauge and noted that it was very near empty. He knew that he would never get the chopper off the ground again unless there was fuel here at the Refuge, whatever the Refuge was! From what seemed like out of nowhere, about a dozen men women came toward the chopper as the rotors came to a stop. There were Vietnamese as well as Americans that were dressed in all kinds of clothing. Some had on shorts with t-shirts, and others were in the uniforms of the countries that they'd come from. Hanger looked at Evers and asked what was going on.

"For the last seven years, I have been building this city I call the Refuge. It's a haven for people disillusioned with the war. They come here to escape and be free."

Before Hanger could respond, a young, beautiful Vietnamese woman carrying an AK47 slung over her shoulder and a nine-millimeter sidearm strapped to her waist jumped into the chopper and put her arms around Evers, kissing him on the lips as tears began to fall from her deep dark black eyes. She spoke to Evers in broken English as she cradled his head in her arms.

"Welcome home. I love you."

Hanger wondered just where the hell he was. The woman was helped by several men, and they lifted Evers off the chopper and placed him in a small cart that was being pulled by oxen. Evers looked at Hanger and introduced him to his friend as Quy Tam. Quy and Evers were joined by several other people, including men and women that were obviously both American and Vietnamese. At that point, Hanger knew that Evers was an important figure here in the jungle, so much so that Hanger thought that Evers was indeed "king of the jungle."

Though in no need of help, Evers signaled to several men and women standing at the door of the chopper to get Hanger and bring him along. Soon, Hanger realized they were all headed deeper into the jungle, and from the looks he was given, Hanger became nervous and couldn't understand what the Refuge was all about and what would happen to him. He only hoped that Evers was truly his friend, though he also knew that Evers had very little respect for anyone but himself. He'd have to trust him one hundred percent; there was no other option.

Fifteen minutes later, the small group came to a very sizable clearing. Hanger looked around, and to his amazement, there were at least twenty or more small houses and dozens of tents. It was a full compound, a village in the middle of nowhere Cambodia.

In the center of the clearing was what looked to be a small hospital, which was where Evers was taken. Quy Tam told Hanger to wait outside and she would come and get him when Evers could have company. Hanger took out a cigar and lit it up, and as he did, an American walked over and sat beside him.

"So what's your story, Lieutenant?"

"Story?" Hanger took a long draw on the cigar and then offered it to the man.

"No thanks, sir, but if you don't mind, I would like to hear what brings you to the Refuge. We have to be very careful as to who gets in here and even more careful who gets to stay. You have to know that the only way out of here, if you don't pass the smell test, is in a body bag. This isn't the United States, and it sure as hell ain't the US Army, so your rank here is worthless. You need to understand that your time here at the Refuge can save your life or end it. The choice is yours. Now if you don't mind, I need to know how you ended up with Evers, and I need to know the truth right now."

Hanger started at the beginning and explained that he had gotten into a fight with his commanding officer after a rescue mission, was demoted from captain, and had gone rogue after that. He explained how he met Evers and had rescued him.

"So you must be the crazy chopper pilot we heard about. Welcome to the Refuge. Anything we can do to show our thanks for saving Evers is yours for the asking."

Evers, truly like the King of the Jungle! Hanger thought. Hours passed, and Hanger had heard nothing about Evers, so he wandered around the Refuge marveling at the array of equipment he saw, which included recreation areas and even a small place that looked to be a bar. Inside were several men and a few women gathered around a table having beers. Hanger decided he could use a beer, as well, and some food.

Behind the makeshift bar was an American. "You must be the pilot of the chopper that brought Evers in. People here just call me Johnny. What can I do for you?"

"Just call me Hungry and Thirsty," Hanger joked.

Johnny smiled and poured a beer. "Hope you like this. It's the only kind we have." He turned around, reached into a refrigerator, and pulled out a sandwich.

"So, what the hell is this place that Evers calls the Refuge?" Hanger asked. Johnny came back from taking beers to the table across the room and then sat down on a stool next to Hanger.

"I'm sure you understand that there are many factors that got this shit war started. Even if those were for good reason, and I ain't saying there were, this war has gotten very political on both sides, and there are thousands of lives being lost for nothing!"

Hanger was hanging on every word that Johnny was saying, and Johnny could tell Hanger was one of those that may have believed in the beginning but was now disillusioned by the ongoing war that to most seemed to be a stalemate even though on paper the United States and its allies were far superior in fire power. "So are you telling me that this place you call the Refuge is a collection of deserters from their posts like me?"

Johnny explained that most were waiting for the war to end so they could return to their homeland. Many had fled the Viet Cong, the North Vietnamese Army, the NVA.

"Hanger, there are people here from all over the world that don't believe the things that are happening here have anything to do with right or wrong. They have lost faith in what their political leaders are saying and want no part of this fiasco. They want to stay here until they find a way to get back to their countries and live a better life, which would be hard to do if they happen to die here."

Hanger looked around and saw dozens of people coming and going with small carts, and even a few US Jeeps. He saw a deuce-and-a-half truck rumbling forward.

"Where does all this equipment come from? And is that actually a hospital with real doctors in it?"

Johnny shrugged. "Enough for now, my friend. You will have to wait until Evers is more alert before you can learn any more. It will be up to him as to how much you should know."

Evers, fucking king of the jungle! Hanger thought again.

As he considered what Johnny had just said about Evers, he realized that even with all his West Point education and training, he was just another dumb shit compared to Evers. *Unbelievable! I should be the king here.*

Hanger knew he was far more educated than Evers. He knew that somehow he would replace Evers as King of the Jungle. What he didn't know was that he was making a fatal mistake. Across the room walking toward him was the woman Evers introduced him to when they got off the chopper. Quy Tam walked directly toward him and sat on the stool that Johnny had just gotten off. "What's the word on Evers?" Hanger asked.

She gave him a steely glance and told him Evers was in surgery to repair the damage to the area of the amputated leg that had been further complicated by the trip from the med surg hospital. It was too soon to know how bad he was and what would be next, but the great doctors here were doing what they could and had high hopes. "You will come with me and for tonight stay in our hooch. In the morning, you will be assigned a place to stay and a job to do as long as you are here." Quy motioned Hanger to follow her.

Hanger looked puzzled. "What do you mean by 'a job'?" he asked.

"Everyone here has to contribute to the greater good of the community," she explained in a patient tone. "You are strong, and those that are do the hardest work. Tomorrow we are starting another living section on the west side of the compound, and you will be given tools that will be used for the clearing of the land. If you prove yourself worthy, you may get to be a crew leader. Time will tell us that."

"And if I choose not to do that, then what happens?"

Quy looked straight into Hanger's eyes. "You will be taken to the jungle, and you will never be seen again!"

Hanger followed Quy and never said another word.

CHAPTER 27

THE WARNING

Lacy and Hank walked into Delany's Pub and were seated at the rear of the restaurant facing the front door. Hank never liked to sit with his back to a door, especially here where things were getting crazier by the day. Yesterday, he had a phone call from his commander in DC at the USAIS informing him that new intel was available that suggested there was a hit out on him. USAIS was going to monitor the chatter and was also sending an FBI agent to the area who would provide additional manpower as well as an extra layer of protection.

Special Agent Simone Ritter walked across the room, and when Hank recognized her, he stood and waved. Hank had met Ritter some time ago on an undercover assignment. He introduced Ritter to Lacy, and as she held out her hand to shake, Lacy couldn't help but notice the stunning good looks of Simone Ritter. She wondered just how special she had been to Hank.

"Pleased to meet you, Lacy," Simone said.

Lacy faked a smile. "Likewise, I'm sure."

Ritter sat opposite Lacy and next to Hank, not wanting her back to the door, either. The waitress walked over and took their drink orders. Scotch neat for Hank, Bud Lite for Lacy, and Jack Daniels and ginger for Ritter.

"We need to take a few private moments to discuss the situation here, Maples, as soon as possible."

"Lacy can hear what you have to say. I trust her. She's in on all the information relating to this issue. There's no need to exclude her."

"And her clearance is at what level?" Ritter asked with a gleam in her eye that Lacy took as a snub. Lacy didn't think Ritter was going to be a friend, but perhaps she could help them solve the pressing problem before it got worse.

"Don't worry yourself over that, Simone," Hank said. "Lacy has been clued in and has been at my side through the last several weeks and even in harm's way a time or two. She can handle herself just fine."

"I'll bet she can," Simone said.

Lacy started to say something when the waitress set their drinks on the table and left the three of them staring at each other.

Lacy waited until the waitress had walked a few feet away and without any fear asked Simone, "And what the fuck is that supposed to mean?"

"Sorry, Lacy. It's been a long day, and I am tired and perhaps a bit on edge. It's not every day I get a message from command that says another agent's life is on the line and get to him fast."

Lacy nodded and thought that she may have misjudged Simone and that they could work together. *What choice do I have?*

Just as they finished their drinks, the waitress returned with another round of drinks. "Compliments from the man at the bar," she said. When they turned to say thanks, the man had already left.

Kent Richards smiled as he got in his truck and backed out of Delany's parking lot. He could only imagine the fun he was going to have killing Hank Maples and the reporter, but only after he watched as Richards killed the woman first. Maybe he might have some fun with the woman before he killed them. He felt his pulse quicken as he thought about the taller, darker woman with them as well. "Maybe a threesome," he snickered. Life was getting better by the hour.

"What happened to man who ordered us drinks?" Simone asked the waitress.

"Not sure where he went, but he left this note with a fifty-dollar bill and told me to give it to you."

Hank opened the folded paper and read it out loud. "Hope you like this drink. It may be your last!" He jumped from the booth and darted out of the door, hoping to catch a glimpse of anyone that may just be leaving, but as he suspected, there was no one out there and no cars on the road. Shit!

"Okay, so what do we know for sure as opposed to what we think is going on here?" Simone asked. "Maples, let's hear from you first."

"So here is what we know. I won't bore you with details but just the essence of what's happening here." He filled her in on the facts as he understood them, including intel that suggested that the drugs that were coming into the country were being shipped by an old enemy from Vietnam who he thought was dead.

"It's hard for me to believe that Ronald Evers made it out of Vietnam. The last I saw of him was in a firefight in Bien Hoa, and he was hit badly. I feel that he must have at least lost his leg and perhaps his life as well. USAIS has never been able to track him after that night almost twenty years ago. I know for a fact that he was a deserter and, furthermore, had deep connections to the drug lords of North Vietnam. He was involved as a leader in the south with a vicious gang of Viet Cong deserters and perhaps several other American deserters as well. I had tracked him down to just outside an air base in Bien Hoa and was engaging him and his men in a gun battle when I got hit in the shoulder. Somehow, he had a connection to another deserter, a lieutenant named Charles Hanger, who rescued him from the jungle in a stolen Huey. I never saw them again."

Lacy told Simone about the attack on the two of them at Lacy's house and the fact that they thought Sheriff Tate was involved as well.

CHAPTER 28

THE MEETING

Tate was drying off after a long shower that he hoped would soothe his aching ribs and throbbing head that he'd gotten at Kent Richards' hands. When the phone vibrated, he saw the screen and knew he would have to answer. It was George Bandy once again pulling the strings.

"Tate. Your office tonight nine o'clock. Don't be late. Richards will be there as well."

The line went dead. For what he hoped would be the last time, Tate thought he might just kill the man and be done with this part of his life. But at the same time, he knew he'd have to deal with Richards as well and knew that wouldn't be easy.

Sheriff Tate looked across the room to the bed and couldn't help but admire the beautiful woman that he was just about to join for some much-needed relaxation. Claire raised the sheets on the bed to reveal her stunning body, and at that moment, Tate decided that he would wait to discuss their future together and the fact that her husband had just hung up the phone.

This was going to be a special night, and in a warped way, Tate was getting even for the bullshit he had to put up with from Bandy to maintain the lifestyle he loved. Claire beckoned with her eyes and her gyrations for Tate to respond, and respond he did. Her breath became rapid as he rolled over and was on top of her still perched on his knees, and as she spread her legs and wrapped them around his waist, he could feel her body heat up as he lowered his lips into the middle of her hips. As he found his target, he felt her tense up as if she was going to explode. She yelled out in pleasure, and it gave him the incentive to explore deeper into her throbbing sexuality. She arched her back to make full contact with his probing tongue.

Claire could hardly stand the ecstasy she was feeling at the moment, and she felt herself releasing her natural juices as she all but passed out. Tate if nothing else was a talented lover, and that was all she needed at this time to escape the fact she was a trophy wife to someone she thought she could endure for the benefits that came with the stature and wealth of her older husband. This, though, was what she enjoyed the most, and under different circumstances, she would trade all that she had for this, but not quite!

Tate got back on his knees and positioned Claire for the final conquest. When he looked in her eyes, he saw nothing but sheer want, and as he entered her, she went stiff with joy and then relaxed as they began frantic movements that seemed to go on for eternity. But in the end, as they both climaxed at the same time, the reality was that as intense as their love making was, it had only lasted a few minutes. As they both caught their collective breaths, they could only wait minutes before they both wanted an encore.

Several hours later, and after a fun-filled hot and then cold shower together, Tate told Claire he had to go and wasn't sure when he would be back. She questioned him.

"Seems your husband and his new hit man Richards want to get together with me and get this shit done with Maples. Seems like that Maples prick and the Lacy Anderson bitch are getting too close to finding out about the reason Ralph died and the source of the drugs that are coming into this area. I would guess you know that good old George is the kingpin here, and not only that, but in this half of the country as well."

Claire didn't want any part of her husband's illicit enterprise. In fact, she was disgusted by him. "Let's just get out of here and go as far away as we can," she said. "I hate that dried-up old bastard and have enough money hidden away that we can go wherever we want and spend all our days doing what we just did and never having another worry in the world."

As much as he would like to do just that, Tate explained to her that in the real world, men like George Bandy and Kent Richards would always be a step ahead of the rest, and their only option was to see this thing through to the end, for better or worse.

"What will be will be," Tate said. "We just have to play it safe until this is over."

Without another word, Tate walked out the door to head for his office and wait for Richards.

CHAPTER 29

A NEW LIFE

Days turned into weeks, and Hanger was indeed working like he had never before, at least physically. He was up at the crack of dawn and fed a meager breakfast of some slop and coffee and on occasion water buffalo. Hanger got the impression that, for whatever reason, Quy Tam was the leader of the compound, perhaps because she was Evers' girlfriend, or maybe she was already that before she and Evers got together. Hanger's only goal at the time was to stay alive and plan to somehow get out of the Refuge. He was making plans to do just that. They had cleared about two acres more out of the woods with machetes and picks and shovels, burning all the waste in big fires. Hanger wondered why no one seemed to bother to worry about being seen from the sky. He guessed it was because the US Command wasn't that close to the Cambodian border.

Hanger was using a shovel and a rake to smooth out an area that would eventually become the base for a wall that would enclose another small cabin-like structure that was referred to as a hooch. After the first night in the Refuge when he had stayed in the hooch that Quy and Evers shared together with Quy's sister Thu Thay, Hanger was assigned to his own hooch. Quy and her sister Thu had brought some water and a plate of what Hanger had begun to call mystery meat. Hungry, he took it gratefully, sitting on the ground to eat. Others around him that were also being served plates of food and water sat down when they saw him do it. He was beginning to look like the leader he was trained to be, just not where he thought he would be doing it.

Hanger had been told weeks ago that he would eventually be told about Evers when the time was right. Now must have been the time, because Quy said, "I have news for you about Ronald."

Hanger would have to talk to the sisters at some point about why it was that their English except for the Vietnamese accent was almost perfect. This place was full of surprises!

"He is doing well and mending nicely," Quy said and followed with, "He will be returning from Thailand soon, and he has been fitted with a new leg at the hospital in Bangkok."

"Bangkok? How the hell did he get there? And why was I not allowed to go with him?" Hanger asked.

Thu Thay smiled at Hanger and said, "You do not understand your place here yet, Lieutenant. It would benefit you to try to learn what it is you have to do to be in the proper place in our society here at the Refuge."

Hanger thought now that maybe Thu Thay was the boss. He would get to know her better in the days and weeks to come, he thought.

Thu Thay was petite, as were most of the Vietnamese women. But something about her fascinated him, including her very muscular build. Secretly, Thu Thay had confessed to her sister that she was thinking fondly about Hanger and wanted to get to know him better. "Maybe he can be my boyfriend," she had told Quy and laughed.

A few more weeks went by, and in the course of time, Hanger and Thu Thay had become close to each other to the point that Thu was living in the same hooch as Hanger. He was indeed finding his place here and learned that Evers and Quy were the leaders of the simple government at the Refuge. He wondered how Quy and Thu were so fluent in English, and one evening after they had eaten and were settling in for the night, Hanger asked Thu and Quy how it was that they seemed so at ease with the English language and the "ways" of the American lifestyle. Quy, being the eldest, explained.

"Before war broke out, our father was a diplomat to the United States and our family lived in Washington, DC, for many years. We went to American schools and college as well."

Thu added that when the Americans invaded the country, their father returned to Vietnam because his service as a general for the North Vietnamese Army was demanded.

"He was a man of great wisdom, and when he had the chance, he defected to the south, but he never made it. He was captured and shot to death by Ho Chi Minh, but not before he made sure that we were safely hidden in South Vietnam. Our mother had died years before, and we have been on our own for many years."

Hanger was mesmerized by the story; the sisters could see it in his eyes. Quy added, "We saw the folly of the situation and came to Cambodia to start this haven for those with like values. Here we strive to make new lives for ourselves and for others who want to create a new and better life for themselves as well."

Thu said to Hanger, "If you continue to learn and contribute, you will be given a chance to leave here a new man in many ways."

Not sure what Thu meant by that, Hanger said nothing and managed a smile directed at both women. Several days later, Hanger learned from Quy that Evers would be coming back to the Refuge that night and was doing well. If anyone knew the next step for Hanger getting out of here, it would be Evers.

Late at night in the sixth week since their arrival at the Refuge, Evers returned to the hooch that he and Quy shared. It was a very tender meeting, much to Quy's relief. She feared he would return bitter from the loss of his leg and would desire to seek revenge, which meant leaving the Refuge.

"It is good to see you, Ronald. I have been worried that you would not want to come to me when you returned from the hospital," Quy said as she wrapped her arms around him. At first, he shied away but just as quickly held her in his arms softly at first and then began to cry.

"What is the matter?" she asked Evers as she held him.

Evers pulled away from her, crossed the room, sat on one of the two wooden chairs that made up almost their entire collection of furniture—a bed and a few odd tables made up the rest of their belongings. He wiped the tears from his cheeks and from his eyes and sighed a deep breath, only to take another deep breath and then slowly let it out in what Quy thought was a sign of tiredness. He looked up at her and said as he patted his artificial leg, "I feel like I am no longer a whole man and am not worthy of your love."

"What you have lost is merely a physical part of you that many men have lost and some even more. What I love about you is what you have in here," she said, pointing to her heart.

It took several more weeks, but as time passed, Evers was getting stronger and was able to walk and even run a bit with his prosthesis, which had been fitted in the hospital in Thailand. He was working out with weights and running at a pace that would be envied by many with both legs.

At the same time, Hanger was becoming increasingly more aggressive and was prone to getting into fights with others in the compound. Thu, though still living in the same hooch with Hanger, was becoming afraid of him and spent more and more time with Evers and Quy. Hanger was also becoming somewhat of a leader to a dozen or so men at the Refuge that had become dissatisfied with the way the overall leaders of the Refuge ran things. The tension in the encampment was becoming a focal point between Evers and those that respected the values established at the Refuge and those discontents that were prone to follow Hanger.

It came as no surprise then to Evers that as the months went by, there needed to be something done to save the entire encampment from falling into what would be a small civil war. Evers was getting stronger by the day, and as he did, Hanger was becoming more irritated by his lack of respect from most of the Refuge. He decided he wanted out!

CHAPTER 30

MAKING A PLAN

The door to Tate's office flung open without a knock. Tate grabbed the service revolver on the desk. When he saw it was Richards and George Bandy, he set it back down.

"What the fuck did you do that for, assholes?" he asked as a small drop of blood ran out of his mouth. He wiped it away with the back of his hand.

"Sick, Sheriff, or just hurting from our last encounter?" Richards mocked.

"Fuck you," the sheriff said. "Touch me again and you're dead."

Richards laughed. "You don't seem to understand, Sheriff. George and I ask the questions and make the threats, not you."

Tate was seething inside and could hardly control his temper, but he knew he had to; he was no match for Richards. As for George Bandy, he knew he could take him. He was much older and feeble, which was why he needed Richards' muscle in the first place. The thought of beating the shit out of Claire's husband buoyed him.

Perhaps I will get my shot, thought Tate. *I'll eliminate Richards and then take the money and the girl.*

"Listen up, Tate," Bandy barked. "This has gone as far as we can let it go. It's time to bring a stop to Maples and Lacy Anderson."

"What do you have in mind, George? I have been watching them and pretending to help them, but so far, they haven't confided in me what they know and what they plan to do. They just keep saying they'll tell me when it's time for me to help."

Richards looked Tate in the eye. "You must be dumber than I thought if you believe that. They're playing you. They either know you're crooked, or at the very least they suspect you are."

"I don't think so," Tate said to Richards. "You just think that because you haven't been able to get to them, either. Neither of you are as clever as you think you are, and if you weren't so fucking arrogant, you might just learn something from me about how to go about true investigation procedures. Oh, and one other thing, assholes. If you take me out, my entire department and the FBI will swarm this town and find out the truth. I can't protect you if I'm dead."

Richards pulled his handgun and chambered a round as he pointed it at Tate's head. Bandy stood and put his hand on Richards' arm. "Not now, Richards," he said. "We need Tate to complete the plan. What you do with him afterwards is up to you, but for now, we still do things my way."

Bandy had all but given Richards permission to kill Tate. *Rock and a hard place*, he thought, but at least for now it appeared that he was safe. He would have to figure out a way to get to Richards when the time was right—if it ever would be.

"There is a shipment on the way that will be the biggest one ever," Bandy said. The drugs would be coming from Detroit, and delivery was scheduled for three days from now. It would have a street value of over three million dollars. Richards and Tate looked at Bandy, and both smiled. Their share of the deal was to be about half of the street value, which meant they would split a million and a half, enough for Tate to get out of Atwood for good. All they had to do was to make sure the transfer was done without any complications and to take them to the dealers on the street.

While it was going to be the biggest amount of drugs they had handled to date, they felt confident they were up to the task. Both

Richards and Tate, though low on trust toward each other, began to run on about how much they were going to take from the deal if all went well. Bandy shut them both up when he held up his hand to bring them back down to earth. "So let me tell you just how this is going to work," Bandy said. "We are going to make sure that Maples and Lacy Anderson become aware of the deal."

"What the fuck are you saying?" Tate asked.

Richards added, "What good will that do and how does that help us?"

"That's why I'm the boss, you assholes. We will set a trap for them with a fake drop off, and when they come to where the shipment is supposed to be taken, we will have enough extra men to make sure they leave with neither the drugs nor their lives. If they bring other cops with them, they'll die, too. Sheriff Tate here can make sure no local cops are involved. Isn't that right, Sheriff?"

Tate nodded but also wondered how they would get word of the drop to Maples.

"It will be your job, Mr. Sheriff, to inform Maples. He'll think you're one of the good guys."

CHAPTER 31

THE SET UP

Maples, Lacy, and Special Agent Ritter ate their dinner and ordered another drink afterwards. After the waitress cleaned the table and set down the fresh drinks, they began to go over the intel that was available, which was coming in almost daily now, concerning a big drug transfer.

"I just want to be clear about something before we proceed," Special Agent Ritter said. "Lacy cannot publish or share any of this with her newspaper until the drug bust is made. She can have the inside story and be at the scene, but we can't have this leak out publicly until all arrests are made."

"Deal," Lacy said without prompting. "All of this is off the record until the case is resolved."

"Okay then. So here is what we think we know at this time. It comes down from USAIS headquarters." Ritter explained that USAIS was involved because it was still believed that military deserters from Vietnam were playing a big role in distributing the drugs that they somehow got out of Vietnam and were planning to sell here in the United States.

"The Drug Task Force has been on alert and is working with state and local law enforcement to try and pin down the exact location and time the deal will go down."

"Who is your source?" Hank asked.

"The local sheriff, Tate. Know him?"

Lacy and Hank snickered. "Yeah, we know him, and as far as we can tell, he might not be the most trustworthy person around," Lacy said. "There have been rumors about Tate for years."

"Rumors? Like what?"

"Let's just say that it may not be a coincidence that major drug dealing is happening on his turf," Hank said.

"You mean the local sheriff is in on the deals?"

"We think it's possible," Lacy said. "That's what I have been investigating some time for the newspaper."

"Well, that being the case, let's set up a meeting with him where we can all be there and see what he has to offer," Ritter said. "If he seems like he's playing games with us, he may not be so eager if he understands who he is dealing with. He might not be as anxious to test the power we have."

They agreed to set up a meeting and let Ritter know when and where it would be.

Tate sat in his office after the meet-up with Richards and was very morose as to how things had gotten so off base at this time. How did running what at one time was a small drug operation on the side get to be this much trouble, perhaps even getting people killed? He wished he had never started in with Bandy. But he was in too deep to back out. *One more deal*, he thought, *and I am out.*

Tate had been given the false information to give to Maples and Lacy Anderson and had put in a call to Maples. When he didn't pick up the call, he left a message to return his call ASAP. While he waited for the phone to ring, he decided to draft his own plan of escape, the probable outcome after the killing of Maples and more than likely Anderson. He had no faith in George Bandy's promise to split the cash with him and Richards. *If I kill Bandy and Richards, I get it all*, he thought.

Tate's phone vibrated; it was George.

"Tate, here's the deal," George said. "If you get this done for us, there will be a bonus for you, and if you don't come through, you have no worries anyway."

Tate knew what that meant, and he knew now more than ever he would need to work hard to escape this situation with his life.

Bandy explained that the drugs would be arriving on the twenty-sixth of the month, and the deal would go down at the abandoned cabin out on Smoke Mountain Road by the lake at two a.m. "The information you are to give to Maples is that the deal will take place there, but at midnight, and you want them to help you set up a trap at ten p.m. so when the dealers get there, they will be in place to take them out. Once we have them trapped in the cabin, we will make sure they never get out. Maples is so fixated on the mission that he will not question your information and will be anxious to finally put this case to rest," Bandy said.

Tate was relieved that it might finally be coming to an end. Whose end, he still wasn't sure.

CHAPTER 32

BREAKING AWAY

CAMBODIA, 1967

Hanger and Evers seemed to be on a collision course, which would do neither them nor the Refuge any good. Evers decided that he needed to have a meeting with Hanger to try to bring calm to the Refuge that was slipping away. They met at Evers' hooch in the absence of the sisters.

Hanger showed up twenty minutes late, and it was obvious to Evers that Hanger had being smoking dope and drinking. As he walked in, Hanger was in a foul mood and stared menacingly at Evers.

"So, what the fuck do you want to talk about this time?"

"Just that, Hanger. Your attitude lately has been less than satisfactory, and the trouble you are stirring up here isn't healthy for the welfare of the Refuge or you, for that matter."

Hanger staggered a bit then sat in a chair opposite Evers. "Tell you what, Evers. Just give me my share of the drug money and half of the drug stash, and I will disappear and leave you to rule this jungle fucked-up place yourself."

"Listen up, you dumbass, and listen good. As of right now, you have nowhere to go, and if you did, you would have no way to get there. The jungle eats people like you for lunch, and if the Cong don't get you, the NVA will. If you get lucky, they will just kill you and not torture you. Further, you have no claim to either the drugs or the money, so it will be in your best interest to settle yourself down for now, do your job, and wait your turn to get the chance to leave once you have done your time here. I will make sure you get out if you want when your time comes."

Hanger stood and on wobbly legs pounded his fists on the table, pointed his finger at Evers, and said, "Fuck you, and for that matter your slut girlfriend and her sister, too. You don't own me, and you can stick this place up your ass. I'm nobody to fuck with, and don't forget, if not for me, you would have died if I hadn't picked you up in the chopper that night."

Evers stood and got toe to toe with Hanger. "I do remember, and I also remember you were late getting there, and because of that, I did almost die. So I hold you responsible, you and that fucking Sergeant Maples."

Hanger took a swing at Evers, but even with his leg still not working one hundred percent, he easily dodged the oncoming fist, twisting to his right and returning a vicious blow to Hanger's face, dropping him to the ground. He barreled another fist, breaking Hanger's nose. As blood poured, the lieutenant passed out.

When Hanger came to, he had no idea how long he had been out or, for that matter, how he got back to his hooch, but there he was still bloody, his face a mess and hurting like hell. He would get even with Evers somehow! He called out to Thu They, but she didn't seem to be there. He looked in the closet, and her clothes were gone. On the table in the makeshift kitchen was a note that simply said that she would not be back and for his own good he needed to stop his irrational behavior if he wanted to live in the Refuge, or otherwise his life would be in danger. He crumpled the note and headed out the door to seek medical help from the small hospital.

Hanger spent the next few days in his hooch alone, thinking of a way to get to the stash of money. He had decided that if he could find the money, he would have enough that the drugs would not be so important, and if he did make it out of the Refuge, the bulky marijuana packages would slow him down anyway. Hanger knew that he had to somehow get back in the good graces of Evers, so he decided to sober up and act remorseful. He would quit drinking and volunteer for patrol. If he could get Evers to trust him for that, he thought he might just have a chance to get out of the Refuge with the money.

A week after the fight, Hanger approached Evers.

Evers was busy behind the hooch when Hanger approached with caution. Evers looked up from his work and stood to face Hanger, who appeared clean and neat and held out his hand to shake.

"I wanted to stop by and see if we could bury the hatchet, as they say. I am very sorry for the way I have been acting and will be on my best behavior from now on."

"What makes you think I should put any faith in what you tell me now that I've seen you at your worst?" Evers asked.

"Because I've gotten off track, and I know that now. I have been a fool lately because of the booze and the drugs. I'm a good man at heart and want to get our relationship back on track. Tell me what I have to do. I have skills that I can use for the betterment of the complex and promise to do all I can to make it up to you, the Refuge, and if she'll have me, with Thu as well." Hanger realized that Evers wasn't going to shake his hand, and as quickly as he had offered it, he let it drop back to his side. He just stood waiting for Evers to say something, anything that would give him a hint that he might get back in the good graces of the King of the Jungle.

Evers turned to leave but, after taking a few steps away from Hanger, turned back and said, "Okay, one more chance, Hanger. But if you fail me again, I will simply kill you. How does that sound?"

"Anything you say is fine with me. Just let me know what I have to do."

"First, you must go and apologize to Thu for the way you have treated her, and to Quy as well. Then prove yourself by going on patrol outside the Refuge."

The Refuge had two types of patrol. One was inside the compound, which was more or less a security patrol, and the outside was for more serious things like bringing back lost or wounded soldiers who had been left behind from their squads. Many were deserting or simply wounded in firefights and left for dead. Another reason for outside patrols was to sell and buy drugs from Cambodian suppliers or local growers then return to camp and get them ready to sell. Oftentimes these patrols ended up in firefights when men were wounded or killed. Evers thought that if Hanger made it back, perhaps he could trust him once again—as much as Evers trusted anyone.

At dusk that same night, Evers approached Hanger, accompanied by five other men, two Vietnamese and three Americans deserters. All were ragged, unshaven, and smelled as if they needed a bath.

"Tonight, you will get a chance to atone for your past actions. About three miles to the west, there will be a group of Cambodian weed farmers with five hundred pounds of marijuana to sell. I trust you with this money to pay for it and make sure it gets back to me," Evers said and then handed Hanger an envelope stuffed with cash. Hanger took a quick look and saw the money was US currency.

He knew this was a test and realized what the Vietnamese men were there to do in case Hanger made a dumb mistake. He was not about to blow this chance to get back in Evers' good graces. The jungle was extremely dark that night, and the only light was from the moon, which was at times covered by thick clouds. Periodically, the small squad of men were engulfed in total darkness, so the going was very slow. Twenty minutes into the short trip, the Americans wanted to stop for a few minutes and wait for the cloud cover to pass, but the Vietnamese wanted to continue so they could get back to the Refuge as soon as possible; they knew the jungle trails well and didn't need light to navigate them. Hanger just wanted to get this trip over with, so when the three other Americans stopped to light up some pot, the Vietnamese started to shout "Didi Mao", Hanger knew from the little Vietnamese he knew, the guides were saying get going. Hanger looked at the three and said that they could light up when they got back to safety of the Refuge, because if there was any enemy out tonight, they might just see the light from the matches, and they would all be in for trouble they didn't need to be in.

Forty minutes later, Hanger and the men came to the edge of a small clearing and could hear the voices of the Cambodians they were supposed to meet. It was obvious that the farmers were getting high from their own product, as they were talking loudly and laughing, all smoking hand-rolled joints. The Vietnamese guides entered the clearing, and the Cambodians immediately raised their weapons. After a few minutes of conversation, the guides motioned for Hanger and the other three Americans to come into the clearing.

The Cambodians walked a few short steps to a pull cart and threw off the cover to reveal what looked like fifty bundles of neatly wrapped marijuana pouches. Hanger went to the cart and with a sharp pocketknife cut open a random few pouches and smelled the contents. He handed the envelope full cash to the farmers, and they began to pat each other on the back and laugh as they pondered their good fortune. The farmers disappeared quickly into the now dark jungle and without another sound were out of sight almost instantly.

The guides pulled out large canvas bags from their backpacks and handed them to the three Americans and Hanger as well, each keeping one for themselves. Hanger got the idea right off and started to pack the fifty ten-pound bags in the sacks, each weighing about seventy pounds.

It started to rain, and the ground quickly began to turn to mud. The weight of the canvas bags began to take their toll on the now-tired men slogging through mud. The three Americans had smoked some weed at the end of the trade off and were talking trash to Hanger and the two Vietnamese guides. Hanger became agitated; he was in charge and didn't want to blow the assignment. Just like in the Army.

"Hey, Hanger," the one called Jack said, and when Hanger turned around, he was looking into the working end of the man's M16, which was pointed directly at his head.

"What the fuck is wrong with you, Jack? What the hell do you think you're doing?" Hanger asked. When the other men raised their weapons as well, Hanger thought the end was near.

"Getting out of here, Hanger. Not going back to the Refuge and that fucking Evers and his bullshit. Me and my two boys here are taking this dope and heading out. You can come with us or you and those two gooks over there can stay here and die. Your choice."

Hanger thought for a moment and looked at the two Vietnamese, who had decided to sit down and wait to see what was going to happen. He could tell by their eyes that they understood more than they let on.

Hanger took the only course of action he had at his disposal and tried to calm the three down.

"And just where do you assholes think you are going if you do leave here with the weed? And what do you think you can do with it if you did?"

Jack smiled a weak, pot-filled smile and told Hanger it made no difference what he said—the only thing that was important right now was whether Hanger was coming with them or was going to die here.

Hanger saw it in their eyes that the dope was slowing down the instincts of the three pot-headed idiots, and he knew it was now or never to make a move on them. Hanger dropped to the ground, spun and rolled over to his left, and at the same time yelled at the two Vietnamese guides to fire. He knew that they understood that much English and only hoped that they would figure out who they were supposed to fire at. In the time it took to blink an eye, Hanger had rolled back to his right and had his own M16 up and fired almost a full magazine at the three Americans, whose eyes were now wide open in shock. When the two Vietnamese began to fire at the Americans as well, the party was over. Two of the Americans were dead and the third was on his knees bent at the waist, bleeding from his leg and his chest. Hanger, now on his feet, approaching the man called Jack, who with pleading eyes looked up at Hanger and begged him to help.

"You know, Jack, this is going to hurt me as much as it will you. Well, maybe not."

And with that, Hanger emptied the rest of the magazine into Jack's chest. He silently hoped that when Evers got word from the Vietnamese guides of what went down, he would once again have the trust of Evers, and if he did, he could start all over in his attempt to get the money he thought he deserved and then disappear.

CHAPTER 33

TRAPPING THE TRAPPERS

S pecial Agent Ritter met Hank and Lacy as they arrived at Sheriff
Tate's office as requested.

"So what do you have for us, Sheriff?" Maples asked.

When Tate saw that there were three of them, he could hardly
believe his luck. He didn't know the other woman, who introduced
herself as Special Agent Ritter. He asked all three to have a seat.

Tate started to explain the plan for next week to take out the
drug runners at a sting. Even though there were several other law
enforcement groups working together, the help of the USAIS would
make the effort foolproof.

"We've just received information that the drugs and the money
exchange will take place on at an old cabin on Smoke Mountain Road.
Our task force will be in and around the cabin a couple hours before,
and we will have them in our crossfire if they decide to try and escape.
We thought you might like to be in on it," Tate said to Hank.

"Glad you're thinking of us," Hank said mockingly.

"I'm not real comfortable with a newspaper reporter being there,"
Tate said, faking concern.

"No worries," Hank said. "She'll be with us. We have an agreement everything is off the record for now."

"Great," Tate said, "but if something leaks out, it's on you."

"I don't leak, Sheriff," Lucy huffed.

Tate offered them a drink, but the trio declined and said they had to get going and promptly did so.

"You know, that offer of a drink sounded pretty good," Lacy said when they were outside. Hank suggested they go to Delaney's.

"Sounds good to me," Ritter said, and with the same breath added, "I'm not sure what to think of Tate's offer to be included in the big bust. Maybe a drink and some conversation in private is just what we need." She fired up the hemi in the Ram truck, and off they sped. Some whiskey, some talk, and Delaney's waited.

They arrived just after seven p.m., so the place was almost empty. Dinnertime was over, and the shift change was getting ready for the evening crowd, which would start to come in around nine, so they could have some quiet time to discuss the situation at hand.

The waitress dropped off the drinks, and as she left, Ritter began the conversation. "First of all, we need to process what we've been told and decide if we can rely on any of it. Personally, I don't have any faith in anything that Tate had to offer, so there must be another side to the story," she said.

Hank and Lacy nodded their heads in agreement. Hank looked at Ritter and said that this whole thing felt like a trap and wondered if Ritter could get more field agents to come to the area and be on hand for any trouble that seemed to be coming their way. "This seems all too familiar," Hank continued. "In Vietnam, where we were chasing a deserter, while we thought we had set a trap for him, we ended up trapped by those we thought were helping us. We barely got out with our lives, and that's how I ended up with this bad shoulder. A deserter named Evers was badly wounded, and that's the last time I saw or heard anything more about him."

"Evers? Never heard of him," Ritter said. "But I will request some more agents and make sure they get here on the twenty-fifth so we can formulate a plan to bring the bad guys down and put an end to this shit. If it is a setup, we'll trap the trappers."

Hank and Lacy, who had been very quiet, both said, "Great," pretty much at the same time.

They finished their drinks, and Ritter got up to leave, throwing a twenty on the table to pay the bill. "I have to hit the phone to the agency, so I will see you tomorrow and let you know what the deal is with the request for more agents." She turned and left without thinking that she had driven the three to Delany's.

Lacy looked at Hank and smiled in a way that he knew meant some late-night adventure was about to make up for what had been mostly a boring day. "You know we have been left here with no ride, right?" Lacy asked.

Hank suddenly realized what the smile was all about. Realizing that his truck was parked at Tate's office, he suggested that they walk to the sheriff's office and pick it up, and he'd take Lacy home.

"Sounds good," Lacy said and then added, "Let's have another drink and talk about an idea that just popped into my head."

Hank had a few ideas of his own tonight, so he ordered two more drinks and waited to see just what Lacy had in mind. He hoped her thoughts were just as spicy as his.

The waitress dropped off the drinks, and Hank asked Lacy what the idea was that had popped into her mind.

"When we go to get your truck at the sheriff's office, maybe we should break in and see what we can find that might help us."

"And just how can we do that?" Hank asked.

Lacy explained that as an investigative reporter, she had experience in getting in doors that were open to her and also some that were not. Then she added, "I may not be the person you think I am."

Tate's office was in the rear of the county building and accessible by a rear alley. The deputy dispatch room was at the front of the building, and no other officers would be around at night. It took Lacy less than a minute to pick the lock with a set of picks, and when the lock clicked open, Hank followed her in and shut the door behind him. Hearing nothing from the front dispatch room, Hank and Lacy opened the door to the main office room. As Lacy went to the desk, Hank headed to a large cabinet in the corner of the room. Neither the desk nor the cabinet was locked, and they both started to search for something that would give them a clue as to the real reasons that Tate was including them in the trap for the drug dealers. Neither of them knew what they were looking for, but both thought they would know it when they saw it.

"Hank, over here," Lacy whispered. "I can't believe that Tate would be so stupid as to leave this in his desk drawer, but I think I just found his game plan for the trap, and we are the bait!"

CHAPTER 34

NOT REALLY REAL

CAMBODIA, 1967

B ack in the safety of the Refuge, Hanger and the two Vietnamese
reported to Evers. When he asked where the three others were,
Hanger started to tell the story, but Evers held his hand up
to silence Hanger and called over the two Vietnamese as well as Quy.
He wanted the Vietnamese to tell the story of the firefight they were
in and didn't trust Hanger fully yet, even though he kept his word
and brought the weed back to him. He wanted Quy to translate the
entire story so he wouldn't misunderstand a single word; though his
Vietnamese had developed in the time he had been in the jungle, he
did not trust in it one hundred percent.

After fifteen minutes of conversation between Evers, Quy, and the
two Vietnamese, Evers turned to Hanger, who was getting nervous
waiting for Evers to say something, and said, "Congratulations on a job
well done, Hanger. Tomorrow we will talk some more about getting
back to a good relationship. For now, go back to your hooch and get
some sleep."

Hanger said nothing but smiled. *This just might work,* he thought
and turned to go back to his hooch. To his surprise, when he got back

to his hooch, Thu Thay was waiting for him as if she was a reward from Evers. Thu looked at Hanger from the makeshift bed as she pulled back the covers to reveal her naked body.

"Welcome back."

Hanger stripped out of his clothing and crawled in beside Thu, and as soon as he did, Thu reminded him of just how much he had come to appreciate her. It had been weeks since he had felt the touch of a woman, and it did not take him long to climax from her sensuous acceptance. After another round of sex, they both fell asleep, smiling.

When Hanger woke in the morning, he smelled food cooking on the open fire that served as a stove and watched as Thu made what looked to be some sort of eggs and meat dish. He would eat well today, at least this morning, and hope for the best the rest of the day. He could start to plan his next step in the theft of the drugs and money on a full stomach, and though he had no time frame in mind, he knew it would be soon, because he didn't know how long he could keep up the façade of turning over a new leaf to impress Evers, even thinking he would take pleasure in killing him if it was necessary. Hanger had not seen Evers for several days and asked Thu if she had seen him and Quy recently. When she answered that she did not know where they were, Hanger got the impression that she really did and was keeping something from him. He started to get angry and thought a sharp slap in the face would make her tell the truth, but he remembered what had happened the last time he lost his temper and didn't want to jeopardize the progress he had made in Evers trusting him again. He knew he would need that trust to make his plan work.

As days went by, Evers displayed increasing trust in Hanger, including opportunities to go into the jungle to buy drugs. In doing so, Hanger was making contacts of his own who he hoped would help him overthrow Evers and steal the cached drugs and the money that was now into the hundreds of thousands. Killing Evers would be a bonus.

On one fateful patrol while Hanger was waiting for the pot farmers to show up, he was startled when from behind him he heard the command, "Halt and place your weapons on the ground and your hands in the air. Get on the ground and keep your eyes forward."

One of the Vietnamese with him who didn't understand English started to turn around to face the voice and instantly was gunned down in a hail of bullets, as was his partner who also turned without heeding what was being said. Hanger, realizing he was now the only one left, did exactly what the voice from behind told him to do.

Unfortunately, Hanger and his small band of rebels had been caught by an American patrol of Green Berets that for some reason had gotten behind the Cambodian border. Hanger knew that it was common for the US troops to infiltrate Cambodia in search of Viet Cong supporters. Face down in the mud, Hanger watched as a pair of boots stood in front of him, and with a swift kick in the ribs, the man in the boots ordered him to stand up.

When he was fully upright and the man in the boots got a look at him, he said, "Who the fuck are you and what are you doing here?"

Hanger quickly decided that he would have to do something rash if he was going to have any chance of getting out of this with his life, let alone with the money and the drugs he was planning on. "Lieutenant Charles Hanger, and am I glad you're here! Been captured by a deserter named Ronald Evers and forced to fly him from the hospital in Vung Tau several months ago. He runs a compound called the Refuge that is a haven for deserters and thugs dealing in drugs to both the Vietnamese and the US Army. If you guys want me to, I can lead you to the Refuge. All I want in return is two hundred and fifty gallons of AV fuel so I can get my chopper back to base and clear up my situation with my commander. He probably thinks I am dead or AWOL."

The leader of the squad looked at Hanger with doubt and decided to check on his status with HQ.

CHAPTER 35

THE DOUBLE DOUBLE CROSS

"Look at these notes, Hank," Lacy said, handing him a notebook with a drawing on it and some names scribbled around the outside of what looked like a sketch of a cabin. She guessed that the drawing was of the Smoke Mountain Road cabin they had talked about with Tate earlier that evening. From the notes and the hastily drawn diagram, it was clear that there was a trap indeed being set as Tate had told them, but not for the drug dealer and his men.

"The trap is for us," she said.

Lacy placed the drawing on the copier, made a duplicate, put the copy in her purse, and placed the notebook back in the same position on the desk as she found it, still shaking her head as she thought about how careless Tate had been, a mistake that just might save Lacy and Hank and at the same time kill Tate.

Hank called Special Agent Ritter, and after the third ring, Ritter picked up. "Ritter," she said.

As soon as she did, Hank started to tell her what he and Lacy had discovered. "So, as I see it, they will want us to be on the tree line to the east of the cabin, and when the time is right, the dealer and his men will enter the clearing from behind the cabin on the west side and enter the back door. Once they enter the cabin, we will be included in the attack and will breach the cabin from the front while the sheriff and the rest of the task force enter from the rear. Only problem for us is the fact that there will be more men already inside the cabin that got there before and also some men that will be positioned outside the cabin but to the far side, setting up an ambush that they think will kill us all."

"Luckily, we have that information and can be waiting behind them and, when the time is right, open fire if we need to, as they will be trapped between you guys and the rest of the field agents I have on call for the night," Ritter said.

"Sounds good to me," Lacy and Hank said almost in unison. They decided to wait for the call from Tate setting it all up.

Ritter, who was with the field agents, headed for the door and wished them all good luck. Hank knew that from his time in Vietnam, they would need all the luck they could get and then some.

"Maples," Hank answered as he looked at the caller ID and saw it was Sheriff Tate.

"I will only say this once and then the ball is your court," Tate said as Hank looked at Lacy and Ritter and put the phone on speaker so they could hear for themselves firsthand what Tate was planning. Hank almost felt sorry for Tate, because he was aware of the false information that Tate was giving him and knew that Tate would soon be trapped in his own lies. The result would be that Tate would end up in jail or worse.

"My team will be about fifty yards from the cabin, waiting for the delivery, and we will also have men in the cabin waiting for them as well. You are welcome to come with us and set yourselves on the east side of the cabin, and when the deal goes down, you will attack with us. We'll have them surrounded, game over!"

"Sounds good to me. And you can count on us to cover you as well," Hank said and added that they would be at the site around nine p.m. to be sure to be in place at the right time.

Needless to say, Hank and the rest of the men Ritter had lined up would be there but far in advance of the time stipulated by Tate. Hank felt confident that Tate would be captured and brought to justice.

George Bandy and Richards met on the morning of the drug deal to work out a few last-minute details they didn't want Tate to know about, mostly because between them they weren't so sure that Tate would survive the night. In fact, they were pretty sure he would not.

"Let's make sure we get what we are going there for. Remember that fucking Maples is mine to deal with, and if Tate gets in the way, he can die as well," Richards said as George poured a glass of bourbon for them both.

"Not a problem for me," George said. "The fewer people that know what we're doing, the better! Just remember the guys that are pretending to be the dealers that enter the clearing are only decoys, and if we need to take them out, so be it," he added.

They clinked their glasses together, and Richards nodded his head at Bandy. As George looked into Richards's eyes, he wasn't sure he trusted him fully. But at this stage of the game, he had no choice. Richards, on the other hand, understood everything!

Nearly an hour before the stipulated time, Special Agent Ritter and the field agents she had requested were set up about fifty yards from the cabin and stretched out in a semi-circle facing the building. She had given all them strict orders of silence even to the point that once they were in place and final contact was made with each other, all communication equipment was to be on mute. She would be the only one authorized to initiate conversation.

Hank and Lacy were wearing sensitive, extremely small state-of-the-art transmitters on them so Ritter and the rest of the small force could hear them and also anything said to them by Tate and anyone else involved. The night air was crisp but not uncomfortable because they all had on full flak jackets and black long-sleeved shirts underneath. The moon and the stars provided ample light as the sky was empty of any cloud cover.

Just about thirty minutes after the agents were in place, Lacy and Hank watched in silence as eight men with rifles entered the area around the cabin and set up a similar perimeter to the one being used by the agents, only about twenty yards from the cabin so they were now directly in front of the agents and would have a direct line of fire to the cabin, not realizing that they were already surrounded. They could be heard laughing because they were confident the trap they were setting for their intended victims seemed foolproof. Ritter smiled. *If those fucks knew what they were in for, they would shit,* she thought.

Tate, Hank, and Lacy entered the clearing and headed to the cabin front door, which Tate unlocked with a key he produced from his windbreaker. Hank had been in many situations similar to this one, and though he was being cautious, he was still alarmed that this bust seemed too easy. He couldn't stop thinking of the last event in Vietnam many years back, and it made him all the more aware of the danger they might be in.

"So what now, Tate?" Lacy asked.

"They should be here anytime now, so we just wait. When we see them enter the clearing, we will fire warning shots at them on my command and try to take them alive." Tate added that if they returned fire, then it would be their duty to shoot to kill. Both Hank and now Lacy as well had firearms and plenty of excess ammo and were prepared to do what they needed to do in that event.

CHAPTER 36

VENGEANCE

CAMBODIA, 1967

The Green Beret team had set up a small camp for the night, and once they got settled, the captain called Lieutenant Hanger over and had the wrist straps that were holding his hands together removed so he could eat some of the mess the troops offered him at the captain's request. The name tag on the captain's shirt said *Reed*. When he spoke, Reed had a very deep and somewhat controlling voice, and the tone was one of concern and at the same time slightly authoritative if not arrogant. It was easy for Hanger to understand why someone so young had gotten to be a captain.

"So, Hanger, or whoever you are, tell me exactly how an American soldier comes to find himself in the Cambodian jungle accompanied by Viet Cong wandering around the jungle in the dark. Make sure I hear the truth the first time. And tell me why my team needs to keep you alive," the man named Reed said.

Once again, Hanger knew he was trapped and that all it would take was a call from Reed to his commander and the truth about Hangar would be known. Surely there would be reports made of the escape and the hostility with the USAIS, and the shoot out with Maples' patrol, the stolen Huey, and the escape from the evacuation hospital in Vung Tau with Evers.

Hanger repeated what he'd already said when captured but with more detail. Reed was unconvinced and skeptical. So Hanger had another idea: he would entice Reed with stories about the Refuge, hoping the captain and his team would use Hanger to guide them there instead of turning the lieutenant in. Surely, Captain Reed would get more kudos for busting up a drug ring and camp full of refugees and AWOL soldiers than merely turning over one AWOL lieutenant.

Reed took the bait, asking Hanger for the location of the Refuge.

"Okay, Hanger, I will let command know ASAP and see what my orders will be. For now, though, you are to be considered under arrest and will be guarded as such."

Hanger listened as Reed tried to reach his command but could only hear one side of the conversation.

"Thunderstorm, this is Rainbow One, do you copy? …yes, sir, Rainbow Six, have a situation that needs cleared up and orders for the future."

After the radio call, Reed motioned for the guard to bring Hanger back to the front of the clearing.

"Seems like you may have left out a part or two about how and why you are in this spot now. My commander checked out a few side notes to your story and was impressed by the fact that you saved the lives of several men some time ago, but not so impressed that you lost control with your commander. However, he sees the good you did and will let you help us figure how to go about taking down the Refuge and this man you refer to as Evers."

It took Hanger almost an hour to tell Reed everything he needed to know about the Refuge and where it was and how to best access it for optimum stealth and with less chance of casualties. Hanger drew a map of how to get there and where the outposts were for the guards, including the schedule that was kept guarding the Refuge, as well as the number of times the outside patrols came and went and at what times.

"Okay, Hanger, thanks for the info. Now you better get back to the Refuge, so if there is anything that changes, you can get back to us. We will have eyes on you at all times, so if you need to contact us, just stop and pretend to shake a stone out of your boot, and we will find a way to get to you. Got it?"

"For sure, but I need one more thing, actually two, from you before we go any further—five hundred gallons of aviation fuel put in the chopper in the jungle clearing I told you about. And I will need you to shoot me!"

"What the fuck are you talking about shooting you for?" Reed asked.

"You have no idea how fucking smart Evers is, and if I walk back to the Refuge after all this time and without the other guys you killed, I'll be dead in minutes. He trusts no one except his girlfriend and maybe her sister. Just fire a round through my left arm so no bone gets broken and then drag me through the jungle for a few yards so I will look the right way when I explain why I came back alone."

Reed looked around the small camp, watching his men listening to the conversation, and raised his eyebrows as if to ask if anyone wanted to do what Hanger asked. As if on a mission, a sergeant with the name on his chest that said *Altomare* stepped forward, took out his sidearm, looked Hanger in the eye, and said, "No matter what you do or say, you are still a fucking deserter, traitor bastard, and if I could, I would put a round between your eyes instead of your arm, you fucker." And with that, he grabbed Hanger's arm, stretched it out, and put a shot exactly where it needed to be.

Hanger dropped to the ground and withered in pain as a medic came up. He pulled Hanger off the ground, took him to the rear of the small encampment, and offered to patch him up. While the rest of the SF team started to laugh, Hanger refused treatment because he didn't want Evers to have any questions about what happened that he wouldn't be able to explain away.

Bleeding, but not too bad, Hanger without the help of the medic cut off the tail of his shirt and made a tourniquet, tied it off, and looked at Reed. As he did, Altomare approached Hanger and the medic, grabbed Hanger by the other arm, and pulled him into the jungle. They were gone for about ten minutes, and when they came out of the weeds, Hanger truly looked the worse for wear. Though he was just supposed to drag Hanger through the field for a bit, Hanger's eyes were beginning to swell shut when they came out. Reed gave a glance around the camp, and not to his surprise, no one seemed to care what Hanger looked like.

As Hanger approached the south entrance to the Refuge, the guard recognized him and sent word to Evers that Hanger was back and alone. Evers had been wondering if Hanger had figured out a way to get out of the Refuge or if he had run into trouble when he failed to return from his last mission. Though Evers was learning to trust Hanger again, he did so with some degree of distrust as well. One thing for sure was, when Evers approached Hanger upon his being brought to the Refuge HQ, Hanger indeed looked the worse for wear.

"What happened to you? And where are the men I sent with you?" Evers asked.

"We got jumped and were ambushed by the farmers. Both my men were killed, and I was wounded and was beaten and left for dead. But when I came to, I was able to patch myself up and after getting reoriented found my way back here. I never thought I would be glad to see your face again!" Without much thought, Evers gave Hanger a pat on the back that Hanger took for a welcome home.

After seeing Hanger and giving some thought to the future, Evers silently decided to start to make plans to get out of Cambodia and figure out how to get back, evidentially, to the States with all the money he had in the stash, now about $600,000, which would allow him to live any way he chose. His nagging desire to find and kill Hank Maples also fueled his ambitions. More than likely, he would take Quy, maybe her sister Thu, too, and as much as he had doubts, maybe Hanger as well.

Evers worked hard to form a network, and the next stop was going to be Thailand, then Malaysia, then South America, and then to the States. A good part of the money would be used for that, but that still left plenty for him to more than just survive. It would be in Malaysia that he would get a new name and paperwork to go with it, after which he would disappear as Ronald Evers and reappear as a totally new person who would then have the freedom to find and kill Hank Maples and, for that matter, anyone that got in his way.

Evers called a meeting with Quy, Thu, and Hanger. He explained that he would be gone for an extended period of time, but not to worry because he was making arrangements for them to leave together when he got back, which would be in five or six days. He left Hanger in charge of the Refuge, and he would be monitored by Quy.

Hanger was both glad and pissed at the same time. Having the trust of Evers was great for his plan and his ego, but Quy could become a nuisance. He had discovered where Evers had hidden his money and drugs and was pretty sure he could get to them before Evers got back, as long as Quy didn't spot him. He decided to leave the drugs and just take the money then escape in the refueled chopper. As much as he would like to take Thu with him, he wasn't sure she could be trusted or would leave her sister.

Under the watchful eye of Quy, Hanger did little to raise alarms. On the third day of Evers' departure, Hanger and Thu were walking around the compound when he started to limp. When Thu asked what was wrong, he told her he must have a stone in his boot. He sat on the ground and unlaced it, pulled it off, shook it upside down, and then replaced it on his foot. It was his signal to Captain Reed. He only hoped that Reed and his men were watching.

That night, after Thu had fallen asleep, Hanger heard a sound outside his hooch that seemed out of the ordinary. Thu stirred in their bed but remained asleep. As Hanger stepped outside to investigate, a hand clamped itself around Hanger's mouth, and with strength he hadn't felt before, he was all but lifted off his feet and pulled into the dark jungle behind his hooch. When he was at a safe distance from his hooch, he felt the hand that had grabbed him soften its grip. When he turned around, the man named Altomare was looking at him; he had his finger up to his lips, indicating for Hanger to be quiet. He could sense that the sergeant would just as soon kill him. Hanger saw no one else until Reed stepped into view.

"So, what do you have for me?" Reed asked. Hanger told of how Evers was planning to leave the Refuge in the next day or two.

"So what do I do next?" Hanger asked.

Reed simply gave the sergeant a quick glance, and as soon as he did, he grabbed Hanger by the back of his shoulder. "I have nothing to say to you, Hanger, but if I were in your shoes, I would be coming up with a plan to get out of harm's way and do it soon," Captain Reed said. "Sergeant, get him out of here now!"

"But what about our agreement for the chopper fuel?" Hanger asked.

Reed scoffed, turned, and walked back to the darkness of the jungle. Hanger was shoved away from the clearing, and as he was, the sergeant drew his sidearm and pulled the trigger. Hanger fell to the ground in a heap but quickly realized he was unharmed as there was no report from the gun. He did however get the message loud and clear. He was now on his own and without a plan on how survive.

CHAPTER 37

SURPRISE, SURPRISE

From their vantage point on the hillside about eighty yards from the cabin, Richards watched as the dealers entered the clearing. Stopping to check their watches, they wanted to be sure they were not early. As they approached the cabin, the only light was from the moon, which seemed almost too bright.

Tate pretended to watch the approaching drug gang as they got within twenty-five feet of the front door. As they called out to the cabin, the door swung open, and Hank, Tate, and Lacy Anderson fired over their heads and yelled, "Drop your weapons and get on the ground!"

Hank saw out of the corner of his eye a flash of light that came from about twenty yards or so from the left of the cabin. He grabbed Lacy and pulled her hard to the ground, and as he did, a barrage of bullets cracked over his head. He thought what his drill sergeant many years ago had told him: "The one you never hear is the last one you ever won't."

He and Lacy dove for cover behind the stone porch. As soon as the first shot was fired from Richards' men, the salvo from Ritter and the rest of the agents' guns opened fire and killed the first four of the eight gunmen right in front of them. When they realized they were trapped between Maples, Anderson, and Tate and whoever was to their rear, they started to throw down their weapons.

It was obvious to Richards that the party was over and he'd been outsmarted. He had depended on Tate to pull off this event and was hoping that he could find a way to have his cake and eat it, too, but that seemed over now that the shooting had ended with most of his men either dead or wounded. Ritter and the rest of the agents started to walk down the hillside, and as they did so, they weren't only looking at the boneheads throwing down their weapons but were being extremely cautious on the way down. Most of them were experienced in this sort of thing and realized that until it was stabilized, it was never over.

Bandy looked at Richards and said, "What the fuck are you waiting for? Kill that fucking loser Tate. If you don't, he will rat us out to save his own skin. Shoot that cocksucker."

Richards looked at the mess down below them and knew that Bandy was right. If Tate was to live, he would be sure to implicate Bandy, who, if pressured too much, would give Richards up to try and save his own ass. But Richards had eyes not only on Tate, but on Hank Maples and the Anderson bitch as well. He thought about all the time he had wanted to kill them all but knew he needed to start with Tate, who if left to live would surely give them all up.

He knew what he had to do and what order he had to do it in. Tate was on the front porch and was clearly out in the open, but Richards had to take the chance moving about ten yards closer so he would be sure to have a perfect kill shot. He knew that he wouldn't be seen too quickly because of the angle to the porch from where he had been hiding. He stood and took aim at Tate's head and squeezed off one round and then another. Tate was dead on his feet before the second round found its mark as well. He crumpled to the ground after falling backwards about ten feet from the impact of the bullets, no longer recognizable as the rounds tore off half his face. As he turned to fire at Maples and Anderson, he was shocked at how fast Maples looked around and located him. Before he could fire off another round, Maples fired several rounds at him, but because of the angle and the darkness, all the shots had missed.

He knew he was way outnumbered. He motioned to Bandy to get going back up the hill to the car. Bandy was out of breath by the time he reached the car. Richards was on his heels and shoved him into the vehicle. He put the car in gear just as Hank and Lacy came over the top of the hill. Richards fired off one round at the pursuers from the car window and roared by, flipping Hank the bird and a grimacing stare. Hank saw another face in the car, too, one he couldn't quite make out.

Lacy got up from where she'd dived to avoid the shot, afraid that Hank might have been shot. Hank looked at her, and all he could say was, "What the fuck!"

Three days later, it seemed like the entire town turned out for the funeral of Sheriff Jimmy Tate, but few knew that the exulted sheriff wasn't a man to be admired. Plans were made to have his service at the local high school in Atwood in the packed gymnasium, which held a couple thousand people. In the rear of the room stood Hank Maples and Lacy Anderson.

Ritter, Hank, and other agents involved agreed not to make Tate's nefarious behavior public. Instead, they would press forward with their investigation and try to find the source of the drug trade that Tate had been a part of.

In attendance were George Bandy with his young wife, Claire. Hank was sure many knew or suspected Claire's affair with the sheriff. But, he thought, it took a lot of guts for the couple to show up.

Pastor Kevin Newell from the New Hope Church talked almost forty-five minutes, touting Sheriff Tate's great service to the community. Then a deputy spoke, vowing to bring to justice the people that were responsible for the death of Jimmy Tate. Attendees gave a rousing cheer after the deputy's speech. Lacy, Hank, and Special Agent Ritter watched with disgust. It was announced that there would be a dinner in the school cafeteria after the funeral was over.

Hank spotted George Bandy and his wife lingering by the side door as the crowd began to disperse. George saw Hank approach and told Claire to wait for him in the car. Claire gave Hank an angry look, and Hank gently said, "Sorry for your loss."

Hank and Lacy, along with Special Agent Ritter, left, headed to Lacy's house for a drink. They did not belong among the mourners. As they sat on the porch sipping their drinks, Lacy asked what everyone was thinking. "What happens now?"

"I don't want to talk about it right now," Hank said. "I have to try and get my mind clear. The other night, when we were at the cabin, I think I saw a ghost!"

A ghost? Now what? Lacy thought.

CHAPTER 38

NOT EVERYONE'S WAR

THE REFUGE, CAMBODIA, 1967

Hanger, Quy, and Thay waited for the return of Evers, and as they did, they talked a lot about how they all had come to be in this odd place Evers called the Refuge. While the sisters still didn't trust Hanger entirely, it seemed to them that his demeanor was changing. Hanger could tell that the girls were trusting him more, a trust he would leverage. He was counting on the Green Beret patrol to help him escape, and that time was coming soon.

Hanger's biggest challenge would be escaping with the money. He had discovered a small cave at the edge of the compound, and though he had not been in there because of the watchful eyes of the sisters, he was confident it was the place Evers kept his stash. He had seen Evers enter the cave, alone, several times.

If his plan worked right, he would go to the cave for money just as the Green Berets invaded the camp. There would be so much chaos, no one would notice him. If Hanger planned correctly, most of the population of the Refuge would either be killed if they resisted too much or taken prisoner if they did not. That included the kingpin, Evers. Hanger also still had hopes that Capitan Reed would come through and the chopper would be fueled up for his escape.

Several more days went by, and Evers was still a no show, so Hanger decided to make the venture into the cave to see for himself if the money was there. Late one night after Thu had fallen asleep and the last patrol went by his hooch, he snuck out. Under moonlight, he made his way to the entrance to the cave. Once inside, he lit his small flashlight, and in the rear of the cave, he found what he was looking for. There were about twenty boxes of various sizes piled in the back of the cave on makeshift shelving. Trying not to disturb the order of the boxes, Hanger gently opened a few of them and counted the money in each. All was US dollars, which he found odd. He did some quick math and estimated the haul to be more than half a million. Carrying all of these boxes of cash alone would be difficult. He'd need to find another way.

After about a week, Evers returned, and with him, he brought news and a new man who he introduced simply as Crow. Crow would be their escort on the first leg of their trip, which eventually would end up in the United States via several stops in between. Crow was an American, and that was all the small group needed to know. The only other information Crow would tell them was that from here the destination was Thailand, where they would be handed off to someone else, who would get them to the next destination, which was Malaysia. From there, eventually they would arrive in South America and then finally in the US. Hanger, Quy, and Thu sat stunned hearing all this. Evers also said that Crow was already paid, as were the rest of the people that would finish the trip. When asked what would happen to the Refuge and the rest of the several hundred people living there, Evers let them know that that would solve itself.

Hanger wondered to himself if Evers knew what he was planning with the SF team based on what he had told them. If so, Hanger knew that he would be dead before the trip began. He still was planning to get to the cave and load the money on the chopper, hoping that Captain Reed would get the fuel he wanted. *Lots of ifs!*

One evening a day or two before they were scheduled to leave, Evers gathered the group and started to tell them why the Refuge existed.

"You know when I was drafted a few years ago, I was just a kid trying to figure out not only what I was going to do with my life, but at the same time trying to understand the world in general. Entering the Army was enlightening, and I really thought I had found a purpose for my existence." He stopped for a few minutes and then continued. "That thought didn't last, though, as I realized that what was being taught in basic wasn't the way things were being done here in this shithole country. The longer I was here, the more I was convinced that the politicians were running this war and not the military."

"I know what you mean," Hanger said. "I was severely reprimanded for saving the lives of a squad of infantrymen and then demoted. Can you imagine that?"

"Hell yes, I can, and what happens out here isn't what the idiots in Washington think is going on! You can see by the mix here in the Refuge that more and more people from all over are disgusted over what they are asked to do. This war is not everyone's war! Shit, I bet that for everyone that says they're fighting for their country, there are three who are just fighting to stay alive and take no joy in killing what is supposed to be the enemy."

Evers went on to explain just how the Refuge came to be when he'd had enough bullshit from the Army and decided to get out any way he could. He promised himself that if there was to be more killing, it would be done for his reasons. Selling drugs to American soldiers, or anyone else who wanted them, was merely a way to finance his endeavor.

"Personally, I think drug users are idiots. And if people want to kill themselves smoking this garbage or shooting up, that's on them. I'm just a supplier."

He justified the drug trade for the ultimate good it produced, which was the Refuge itself.

"People come here, and some are able to get out safely and others have died here, and no matter what I do, the Refuge or other places like it will continue to exist until governments learn the value of becoming partners rather than political enemies. You may not understand this, but those of us who chose to not fight that war are fighting a war nonetheless and have our heroes as well. Some of those heroes are buried here."

Hanger slipped away in the early morning hours, went to the cave, started to transfer the boxes of money into sacks, and then carried them to the chopper. He restacked the boxes neatly, first filling them with bamboo in case Evers checked his stash before the Green Beret raided the camp, which would be just a couple days away.

Captain Reed had requested four platoons of Special Forces and was granted his request. With almost two hundred men well equipped with all the weapons they needed, he was sure that he would be able to take the Refuge with little effort. His hope was that if Hanger was right about who the ringleader was, he would capture Ronald Evers and bring the traitor to justice. If things worked out right and Evers gave him trouble, he would save the time and trouble of a lengthy court martial by killing Evers outright. Nothing would make him happier!

As zero four hundred approached, Captain Reed and his men were staged to the north and to the west of the Refuge as to not be caught in a crossfire. The animals in the jungle had stirred at their approach, making the night unusually noisy.

Evers was restless that preceding evening and had gone for a walk to calm himself. The surrounding jungle didn't sound right, nor did it feel right, he thought. He felt paranoid, which triggered his sixth sense of ensuing danger, an instinct that had saved him many times in the past.

Evers gathered the sisters, Hanger, and Crow and gestured for them to follow. They were heading in the direction of the cave and were now just outside the boundary of the Refuge. Hanger had a sick sense that something was wrong and asked Evers where they were headed.

"To the chopper that you flew us here in!" Evers replied.

"It's out of fuel, remember?" Hanger replied.

"Not anymore," Evers said. "But first, I need us to gather some boxes I have stashed in a cave."

Just then, the roar of gunfire erupted behind them. The small group hit the ground and took cover.

"The Refuge is being invaded. Forget the cave. We need to get the hell out of here. We're going to the chopper!" Evers bellowed.

Hanger swallowed hard. Either way, he was screwed.

At first, the SF troops stormed the compound and met with little resistance, but then those they were trying to capture calmed and decided that it would be a fight to the end. Oddly, the Americans, Canadians, and the rest of the deserters along with the Viet Cong were now fighting side by side against a common enemy. They had the protection of their hooches, which at that point became like defensive bunkers. It was surprising to Captain Reed, and for that matter the rest of the platoon leaders, that they were as well armed as they were.

From the northwest corner where the invasion started, Reed took one platoon and headed around the perimeter of the compound, hoping to get behind the resistant enemy. As they rounded the south side of the compound and got behind the enemy, Reed motioned to attack. Then without warning, they found themselves setting off booby traps, and as the first of three men fell mortally wounded, Reed decided to back the rest of the men in his command away from the hell that was being thrown their way.

At the same time, the other three platoons were continuing to push hard at the center of the Refuge, and the men and even the women that were fighting back started to take more and more casualties to a point that many were starting to put up their hands and throw down their weapons. As they did, many of the SF men continued to fire at them anyway and cared less when most of them began to beg for mercy. At the rear of the compound, Reed had regrouped his men and could see what was happening on the other side of the compound, and though he would later berate those that kept firing, he would do so only in gesture. The last of the enemy fighters that faced Reed and his platoon slowly started to give up, and they also threw down their weapons.

Altomare had been hit in the lower leg and, though in some pain, was more pissed than anything else. He swung around and emptied the last clip of his M16 into the group of men that, for the most part, were unarmed, killing or at least injuring as many as he could before Captain Reed tackled him and pinned him to the ground.

"Enough, Sergeant, enough!" Reed shouted, to which the rest of the squad could hear him say to the Captain, "Fuck you! Oh, excuse me, fuck you, sir!"

Reed and the rest of the SF troops rounded up the survivors of the Refuge and herded them out to a clearing in the jungle that had been set up as a Huey landing zone. They forced the deserters to sit back-to-back on the ground until they were evacuated back to Vietnam soil and then to prison camps.

"Any sign of Evers or Lieutenant Hanger?" Reed asked a platoon leader.

"No, sir. We checked their hooches. Looks like they got out before we got here."

"Damn," Reed said. "Those two are slippery bastards. I wonder if they headed to Hanger's Huey."

Reed ordered his troops to set the compound on fire and burn it all to the ground.

Reed was disappointed that Hanger was nowhere to be found nor was Ronald Evers. They, Reed thought, would be fair game at some future point. From their vantage point, now about a mile from the Refuge, Evers and the escapees could hear the loud explosions and see the smoke now rising from the area that used to be their home. They had bypassed the cave and headed straight to the helicopter. Evers figured he could come back to fetch his money later.

It was obvious now to Hanger that Evers knew he had tried to steal the money, but at the same time, he thought Evers needed him to fly the chopper if indeed it was fueled up. As the Huey came into sight, Evers came alongside Hanger and put his arm around Hanger's shoulder. "Thanks for saving me the time to transfer the money to the chopper. I really was starting to trust you again. You know that, don't you?"

Hanger didn't know what to think at this point and thought that anything he said might make things worse for him, as if that was possible. The only thing that gave Hanger hope of living through this was his ability to fly them all to safety; after all, he was the only one that could fly the Huey. Evers gave him a wink. "Let's get the hell out of here while we still can."

Hanger buckled into the pilot's harness in the Huey, and Thu sat by him as Evers, Quy, and Crow got in the back section and also buckled up. Looking at the gauges, it was clear that the chopper had indeed been fueled, so without hesitation, Hanger started the engine and waited for everything to warm up. Thu put on her headset, as did Hanger and the rest of the passengers.

Once they were all in communication with each other, they did a sound check, and all could hear and speak to each other. Thu smiled at Hanger and sat as close to him as the harness she was in allowed. Hanger felt in control for the first time in a long time and realized that Evers needed him now perhaps like never before.

"So how is it that this chopper has fuel, my friend?" Evers asked Hanger over the headset. It was a question that Evers knew the answer to.

Crow has been paid well, and one of his tasks was to make sure the chopper was fueled and ready to go.

Hanger was at a loss for words as he could not tell Evers that the Green Beret team had done it as a favor for him telling them all about the Refuge. Or had they? Was this something else that Evers knew about and Hanger didn't? Thu nestled even closer to Hanger and put her arm around him as if to protect him from any harm Evers may think to cause him. Hanger kept quiet as the engine started to smooth out, and lift off was just a minute or two away.

"I'll bet you think it was your SF buddies doing you a good turn for helping them find the Refuge and take it down, don't you?" Evers said, and because of the headsets, they all could hear the conversation.

At that point, Hanger knew he had nothing to lose and said, "Listen up, you fuckhead. The Refuge was about to be overrun with or without my help, and if you had been smarter rather than such a dumb fuck, it might just still be there. Furthermore, I am the only one that can get this Huey off the ground and get us out of here before the SF patrol finds us, so for now fuck off and let me do my job."

Hanger felt what seemed like a spider bite at first but thought nothing of it until he felt dizzy. He watched as Thu pulled her hand away, holding a knife, and he saw the blood pouring down the front of his shirt. He tried to say something, but the blood was also filling his throat, and the words were garbled at best. His vision was starting to blur as life was leaving his body. He looked directly at Thu, and she smiled. The last thing he heard was Crow unbuckling his harness, and he felt himself being pulled out of the pilot's seat. He was dead before he hit the ground.

Had he lived, he would have heard Evers say to Crow, "Let's get this thing off the ground. One fucker dead now and one to go!"

Crow hopped in, put on the now-empty harness, and with a seasoned pilot's expertise lifted the chopper off the ground, turned the nose of the Huey south, and headed for the next stop. From his vantage point above the SF units below them, Evers resisted the opportunity to use the onboard door guns and strafe the men that had just destroyed the entire compound called the Refuge. It was a rare weak moment for Ronald Evers.

CHAPTER 39

NOT REALLY
A GHOST

"What did you mean you think you saw a ghost?" Lacy asked when everything had calmed down a bit. She and Hank were having a second drink on the porch of Lacy's house after the funeral and Ritter had left for the evening.

"I'm not sure myself, Lacy, but I thought I saw someone I thought was dead in Vietnam."

Hank thought he had mentioned the incident in Vietnam many years ago when he was on assignment chasing a deserter and drug dealer named Ronald Evers.

"I remember you telling me all about it when you first came back to Atwood, but what does that have to do with what happened last week?"

"I might be crazy, and sometimes I think I am, but I thought I saw Ronald Evers in that car!" Then he added, "I felt sure that when the shooting stopped that night, I saw his leg all but off his body, and they were at least a thirty-minute flight to the evacuation hospital in Vung Tau. He would have bled to death by then. I must have been seeing things that were not possible."

Lacy had read about PTSD and thought to herself maybe she had just experienced it with Hank. She decided to ask Hank if he thought it could be that. "Hank, do you think that when all the shooting started, you could have had a flashback to that time in Vietnam you've talked about before and just thought it was him?"

"I don't know, Lacy. It just seemed so real that I want to think that somehow he survived and is back here and that's who we've been chasing. What's more, and not impossible to believe, is that he may be hunting me as well!"

"That's ridiculous. Why would he, if it is him and he did survive somehow, want to find you?"

"Not as ridiculous as you might think. If he did survive, he might just have a vendetta to satisfy against me after all these years. Some people are short on common sense but long on hatred and vengeance."

Hank became uncomfortable talking about the subject and suggested they finish their drinks and hit the sack. He needed a good night's sleep. He finished his drink, and with little left on his plate, he said goodnight to Lacy. He went to the cupboard, pulled out a blanket, went to the couch, covered himself up, and was asleep before Lacy came in from the porch.

Lacy came in shortly after, looked down on the sleeping Hank Maples, and wondered if she had gotten herself into a situation she wasn't capable of handling. She bent over and kissed Hank on the forehead, went to the bedroom, and like Hank was fast asleep within a very few minutes. Tomorrow would be a day filled with questions that needed answering as soon as possible.

In another part of town, another meeting was underway. George Bandy and Kent Richards were trying to come up with a plan that would keep the federal agents at bay while they decided whether to give up the drug business since Tate was dead now and it would be a long shot if they could bring someone that George could trust to give him the help and protection Tate had offered all these years up to speed. Bandy didn't think he had the time or energy to start over. One thing he did know was that Kent Richards was not to be trusted with too much information or, for that matter, much else.

Unlike Tate, Richards was proving to be too independent. George had also become very leery of Richards' actual motive for hanging around and wasn't sure, but he felt he needed to let Richards know that he was through with this illegal endeavor. He feared what Richards would do if he told him he was no longer needed. *Richards needs to go,* George decided, *and fast.*

One loose end was George's wife, Claire, and her openly secret affair with the now-deceased Tate. George had never let on that he knew about Tate and Claire's relationship, but he had, and it bothered him. But he needed Tate, and Claire was a way to keep a leash on the sheriff. Plus, he could no longer fulfill his much-younger wife's sexual needs, so Tate effectively took pressure off George to perform. It was a sordid but convenient arrangement that had run its course. Tate's death was certainly bad for business, and now George Bandy had no practical use for his wife. Maybe he would have Richards do one last job—kill Claire. The life insurance payout on her would be icing on the cake.

As for Claire, she knew she was on thin ice with George, as it became evident by his tone and demeanor. She suspected he was behind Tate's death and began to fear for her own life. She concluded what George had—she was no longer needed. She decided to get as far from Atwood as she could and do it fast.

George Bandy pondered his dilemma a few days and decided to quit while he was ahead. He had to let Richards know and was a bit leery of just how to go about telling him without offending the man who seemed ruthless.

George summoned Richards to his office. When Richards sat down at the mahogany desk, George pushed a leather-covered briefcase across the spacious desk and said, "Richards, this is for you. I'm sure that when you look inside, you will see that there's more in there than we agreed upon when we first met."

Richards opened the case, and while he tried to look calm, he almost lost his composure when he realized that George did indeed not only honor his commitment but had far surpassed it. They had agreed upon one hundred thousand dollars to take care of Tate and Hank Maples and to protect George from harm's way. Even though the job was only half done, Richards counted $200,000 in the briefcase. Bandy felt that if he gave Richards enough cash, he would just go away. After all, there was enough money stashed away to live two lifetimes, and at his age, George would never need that much. And he no longer cared about leaving an estate rich enough to preserve his wife's lavish spending. *Screw her!*

Richards got up from the desk and stuck out his hand to shake with George, a gesture he rarely practiced. For Richards, the handshake was the beginning of the end for George.

CHAPTER 40

A NEW LIFE

For the money Crow was paid, the path to the United States for Evers was already set, and all that needed to take place was time and perhaps some luck. Crow had prearranged places to land the stolen chopper and get refueled. He had also arranged for many palms to be greased to get Evers and the two sisters from Thailand to Malaysia.

On the first leg of their escape, Crow set the chopper down in a very desolate area called Phu Quoc, which wasn't too far from the border of Cambodia and South Vietnam. A fuel truck arrived on time. They would spend a few hours resting there and then at dusk fly off over the Gulf of Thailand on the way to Malaysia.

"What is so important to you that nothing else matters other than you getting to the United States?" Quy asked Evers as the four got out of the Huey and took a much-needed break in their journey. They had wandered off and sat under the shade of a tree while the chopper was refueled and the refueling crew ran checks on the rest of the chopper's systems. No stone was unturned in that effort as Crow knew he had only one chance to get this job done the right way. One mistake and the entire mission—and for that matter the events of the last several years—would be for naught! There were no second chances.

Evers looked at Quy, and as he did, he patted his artificial leg and said, "The man who did this is there, and he has to pay. I have felt as half a man since this happened. I want to look him in the eye just before I kill him and watch as the life leaves his body."

"But there is so much else that you can do with all the resources that you have at your disposal," Quy pleaded. "Why not just forget that part of your life and stay here with me and we can build a great life here when the war is over?"

Evers looked Quy in the eyes, and in them he could only see her love for him.

"I would love to do that, Quy, but for me, the war will never be over no matter if it ends today."

Evers turned and looked out over the fields that lined the shore of the gulf, and while it was as beautiful as Quy herself, he couldn't see any way for him to enjoy it.

"They will hunt me down until one day they find me, and at that time, there will be death, and more than likely it will be mine. I have decided that if that is to be my end, I choose to be the hunter, not the hunted. I will have my pound of flesh, and that will be Sergeant Hank Maples."

With that, Evers picked up Quy, carried her into the jungle, and made love to her as if it would be the last time. She responded and hoped that it wouldn't end here.

Crow had arranged for a warm meal that was enjoyed by all; they had eaten nothing since the fall of the Refuge, many hours before. Crow signaled to the rest to board as the sun was setting over the coastline and started the engines. While the Huey was warming up, the sisters approached Evers, and with heads slightly bent, both handed him a small bouquet of handpicked flowers.

"What is this?"

"It is our goodbye," Quy said. "We cannot go with you. You have a death wish, and with all the death and terror here in our homeland, we do not care to be part of it anymore. We wish you well in your quest to destroy but wish to have no part in it."

Evers thought for a moment as a tear trickled on his cheek. "But Quy, I have much to offer you once we get back to the United States and I do what I have to do. If all goes well, we can come back here and live a promised life or go anywhere we want. With the money I have, we can start a brand-new life."

Quy flashed that dainty smile that all but melted Evers' heart, and then she and Thu turned and walked toward the jungle. Before entering the darkness, she turned back around and with a pained look in her eyes said, "If that is to be, then I will be here when you return."

And with that, she and her sister walked out of the clearing and into the darkening jungle.

At that point, Evers had never been so unsure of himself.

Crow was warming up the engines of the Huey as Evers returned to the chopper and motioned for him to lift off. "Where are the sisters?" he asked.

"They're staying here. No more questions, just go."

By the time Crow was headed out over the gulf to northern Malaysia, Evers was fast asleep. The three hundred miles to the next landing zone and prepaid fuel stop would signal that Evers was well on his way to his new life. He slept soundly and without remorse.

As Crow descended in the stolen chopper toward the landing zone, Evers stirred when he felt the drop in speed and altitude. The constant drone of the chopper rotors had provided a beat that kept him asleep for the entire trip. Once on the ground, a crew approached, driving a deuce and a half truck with a five hundred–gallon bladder of AV fuel. As before, they had food with them. The crew worked quickly, and within the hour, Crow and Evers were ready to set off for the last leg of the Malaysian trip, and there they would rest for the night.

CHAPTER 41

THE RECKONING

George had requested a meeting with Hank, and when he came to meet, he brought along Special Agent Ritter and Lacy as well. Bandy had decided to seek the help he needed in dealing with Richards, and in doing so, he thought he would be able to deflect any effort there was in identifying him as involved in the drug dealings if he could somehow implicate Richards as the leader of the syndicate running the drug operation. Bandy had no idea that the agents had a suspicion that Bandy was involved. He had a plan, and now was the time to get it going! It seemed to him it was now or never with his distrust and perhaps a little fear of Richards.

"So what is it that we can do for you?" Ritter asked when they all had taken a seat around the large conference table in George's office.

"As you may or for that matter may not know, I am involved in many kinds of businesses, and as such, it is important for me to know many things about anything that might affect the way I proceed to accomplish my goals. To create a vast empire in all parts of the world, much knowledge is necessary. I have a team of investigators who have reach to almost anywhere in the world. For this conversation, that is all you need to know about that for now."

While he was saying all that, Ritter, Maples, and Anderson looked at each other in a curious way as if to question why he was telling them this here and now. Maples took the lead. "So what is it exactly you are getting at and why is it important to us?"

"The man who killed Sheriff Tate is still around here, and he has control of the drug operation in this part of the country. He wants to kill you as well, Maples. It's almost as if he has a vendetta against you."

"So just how do you know all this? And who is this person you refer to?" Hank asked. "And why do you think he has a thing for me?"

George didn't answer the question. Rather, he continued to talk in vague terms about Kent Richards and his possible motivations.

"I'm telling you this because you're in danger," George said. "Perhaps between us we can not only get the drug flow stopped but kill Richards as well."

Hank made another mental note that Bandy had said kill rather than capture. Odd that he would think that way, he thought. Maybe there was something he was trying to hide that would die with Richards.

At the same time George Bandy was trying to sell out Kent Richards, Kent Richards was having a drink with the very alluring Claire Bandy at a hotel bar in Cold Water City, about ten miles outside of Atwood. Claire was sure no one knew her there. She hoped Richards might kill her husband, freeing her from the old man so she could inherit his estate. She knew she had signed a pre-nup, but also knew if she could get him killed, she could steal all she needed before probate would even start. All that she knew about Richards was what Tate had told her—he was a killer working for George.

She watched Richards sip his drink, his eyes twitching.

"You seem agitated, Kent," she said.

He glanced at her and then looked away. Outside, the sun was setting.

"Just old nervous ticks from my time in the service. I just never have gotten used to dusk. It seemed that when something bad happened in Vietnam, it was always just about dusk that hell would break loose."

"So you were in the Army? What did you do? What was your job?"

"Maybe when we become better friends, I'll tell you more about myself," Richards said, signaling his interest in her. He was getting aroused by the thought of being with her.

"You're a very interesting man, Kent Richards. A woman like me would have a lot to offer if you played your cards just right." She leaned closer to him and kissed him on the lips.

At first, he pulled away but quickly gave up as her tongue searched for his and her teeth bit softly on his lip. Richards, not the fool she thought him to be, pulled away, though hesitantly, and as he looked in her eyes, he lifted his drink and took a sip as if to let her know he would be the one making decisions tonight.

"And, with the exception of the promise of your body, what else do you have to offer?" Richards asked with a smirk on his face. Claire took a wild swing with her right hand at his face; he caught her hand mid-air and squeezed. Claire showed no fear, grinning flirtatiously and then submitting to his strength. He smiled back, and they both relaxed, summoning the waitress for another round—Scotch for him and a gin martini for her.

"To answer your question, Richards, I have access to large sums of money that George has hidden away from all the illegal activity he does. He thinks he hid it well but not as well as he thinks. If you want to help me get away from George, I can bring that as well as, to use your words, the promise of my body. I'm quite sure you will not be disappointed!" If nothing else, Claire was very good at what she did, Richards thought, and rightfully so; he had nothing to lose. His mind was racing. The break of his life had just fallen into his lap. He was in a position to kill Hank Maples, securing his vendetta, kill the man who had hired him to off Tate, then take the guy's wife and money.

I just hit the lottery, he thought.

They finished their drinks and secured a room in the hotel. They took the elevator to the fourth floor and entered the room, barely able to keep their hands to themselves. At first, they both were very tentative, but as the seconds passed and turned into minutes and ultimately hours, their inhibitions left, and there was an animalistic action to their sex. Claire, wanting to take control of Richards, knew exactly what she needed to do, and Richards was equally aware of his demands. The two were in ecstasy and then agony until very early in the morning when both rolled over on their backs and fell asleep.

As great as the night and the sex was, Richards knew that it would be the last time he and Claire would have such a night. Claire, on the other hand, was convinced she had gained the power over Richards that she would need to escape with her life from the chains she was feeling from George Bandy. She would be free at last!

CHAPTER 42

JOURNEY HOME

MALAYSIA, 1967

Crow landed the chopper for the last time, as the two would be parting company very soon. As agreed, Crow would wait to be sure the men he had engaged to meet them and get Evers off to the final destination would show up as scheduled. Evers had been through a lot to get to this point and was expecting to have an easier final leg of the trip that would wind up in the rocky mountains of West Virginia. From this point on, he would become a different man with a new identity and passport, though forged and paid for with the money Crow had been given, and it would allow him to travel the rest of the way with little danger of being caught. For now, he and Crow would enjoy the next few days on the shore of the South China Sea engaging with the eager young women looking for their way out of poverty and trying to find their place in the hearts of young men.

Crow had arranged for Evers to meet with some men who would be able to create an entire new profile for Evers, who would become someone entirely new with papers to prove his existence now and even for years past. Here in the back rooms of Malaysia's underground, it was no different than many other elicit places in the world. Ronald Evers in just a few short days would cease to exist, and a brand new man would be introduced to the world.

Crow had become somewhat of a savior to Evers, and he wanted to reward him for his work. Though he had been paid plenty when they first struck a deal in Vietnam and Cambodia, Evers thought he needed to pay Crow even more. Then again, he could not get past the thought that Crow would also be the one link to his past.

Crow took Evers to a pre-arranged meeting place in the back room of a local bar oddly enough based on what they came here for called The Exchange. The smoke-filled room was spacious and included a bar of its own and was filled with people smoking, drinking, and gambling.

Crow introduced Evers to a rather large Asian man who must have been six foot four inches and tipped the scales, Evers thought, at least 240 well-put-together pounds, rather large for a man of oriental origins. Amed looked at Evers with a menacing leer that was meant to show anyone looking just who was in charge and why. Leaning against the wall on either side of the room about six feet away were two other even larger men, who watched Evers with the same hard look. In very broken English, the man named Amed smiled and in a gentle voice said, "So, you are Ronald Evers. Welcome to the last day of your life."

Evers was a bit startled by what Amed said, so much so that he almost reached for the sidearm he was wearing in the small of his back. But a glance at Crow, who was smiling, gave Evers a new sense of calm. Besides, he realized, if Amed wanted him dead, he would already be so.

"Sit here and let's get to know each other for a few minutes," Amed said, pointing to an empty chair at his table. Evers sat, and as he did, a young woman approached the table with a bottle of some sort and poured him a glass and then refilled Amed's.

"To your good fortune and to your new life," Amed said as he tossed the entire contents of his glass down his throat. Evers took a sip; it tasted awful, like a burnt log. Amed raised an eyebrow, so Evers, not wanting to insult his host, gulped the rest down.

Amed laughed, as did the two bodyguards against the wall. Crow smiled as he watched what was going on.

"Fuck that shit, whatever it is. Let's see the paperwork I came here for." He had used a rather abrupt tone, and as he did, the bodyguards snapped straight up. It was clear to see that they were about to raise the weapons that had appeared almost out of nowhere. Amed raised his hand as well but with his palm down, said something to the two men that caused them both to assume the posture they were in before.

"It is with much urgency you must have that would cause you to offend your host. Not a very respectable way to start your new life," said Amed, smiling. He snapped his fingers, and a young woman approached the table and handed a folder to Amed. He opened the folder and looked through it carefully then handed it over to Evers.

"Welcome to your new life, Mr. Kent Richards!"

Evers was stunned by hearing his new name and was overwhelmed by the perfectly crafted documentation that was before him. He had paid dearly for this new identity, but with the amount of material he'd been given, he felt it was money well spent. Picture ID, passport, driver's license with an address in West Virginia, Social Security card with a number on it that must have been from someone recently deceased or perhaps disappeared. There was also a DD214, which showed that Evers, now Richards, had served in the United States Army and was honorably discharged. Evers was now very sure of the fact that he would be in the States soon and would find Maples and repay him for what he had done. In the folder as well were travel vouchers that would get Richards back to the United States.

Amed raised his glass, and the young women that had brought the first round returned and poured him another. He glanced at Richards as if to offer another, but Richards and Crow were standing up and with a casual wave declined to have another. Amed and now the bodyguards laughed and waved goodbye as well. With the folder tucked into his jacket pocket, Kent Richards and Crow walked out of the Exchange into the night and headed back to the safety of the chopper, where they planned to spend the night at the camp Crow had set up.

Crow sat across from Richards and said, "Well, I guess this is where we part company, Kent Richards. Good luck getting back to the States. With the paperwork you have, it should be a done deal. I'm sure Maples will be surprised when you finally find him and give him what he deserves."

"I want to thank you for all you've done for me, Crow. I wouldn't have been able to get this far without you."

Crow smiled and started to say thanks, but just as he was about to talk, his eyes widened as Richards' 9mm appeared out of nowhere and pointed directly at his head. Crow never heard the shot that killed him.

Richards placed the 9mm back in his waistband and turned over on the mat to catch some sleep he would need to start the long trip back to the USA. No more links to his past!

CHAPTER 43

CLAIRE

Claire knew what she was capable of. As she looked at Richards, she thought of her life and how she happened to be here at this place and at this time and how she had promised herself years ago to always be in charge. If nothing else, she was an opportunist. She would control him soon!

She was a product of an unloving home in which her mother was a woman with loose morals and a father she never knew. On more than one occasion during her childhood, her mother would bring home one man after another, and she was relegated to her room so her mother could entertain her current lover. Her mother, Marie, was a beautiful, full-figured woman that any man would give his attention to, and Marie was always eager to use her sexual allure to get what she wanted. It was no accident, then, that Claire assumed that that was the way it was supposed to be. As Claire matured, it was common that when Marie's many different men tired of her, they would turn their eye towards Claire. Claire was blossoming into a very beautiful young woman with a stunning body that she was learning to use to her advantage. On more than one occasion after a satisfying evening with Marie, some of the men would see Claire and in an unsavory way entice the young woman to join in the fun. For the most part, Claire would spurn their efforts, but now and then at her mother's urging, Claire would consent to a sexual encounter with her mother's lovers, much to the delight of her mother's desires.

With no real money to advance her education, when Claire graduated from high school, and for that matter she had accomplished little academically speaking, she worked in several menial jobs around Atwood. When nothing better happened, she took a chance and for a short time moved to Florida with the thought of finding a new life away from the horrible environment she found herself in. In Florida, working in a local pub in Naples, she began to understand that she indeed had something special to offer to enjoy a great life: her body. At first, she had no real idea what direction her newfound success should take her, but after spending time with many blowhards, she began to realize that if she wanted to have any real chance of living a charmed life, she needed to focus her efforts on the right type of men. She was quick to realize that the one thing most men wanted, particularly the most successful, was a woman that would be a compliment to their egos. Claire with her stunning good looks and her loose morals fit that criteria like not many women did.

Claire became a woman with an unrealistic view of her life. For a long period of time, she became involved with a man named Tyron who at first seemed to be different than the many other men she had become involved with who, as soon as they tired of her, would replace her easily. Tyron at first spoiled her with gifts and took her on short cruises on his sizable yacht. For a short time, Claire thought she had finally found a life that she felt she deserved. It was on one of the trips from Florida to the Bahamas on the yacht that she realized she was once again being used for her body. Halfway to the island, Tyron stopped the boat, and when Claire asked if there was a problem, Tyron said that the three men he had brought with him wanted to have their way with Claire.

As outraged as she was, she felt she had no choice in the matter but to give into his demands. She was afraid that if she didn't, he might just toss her overboard. Since no one really knew where she was and what she was doing, her disappearance would go unnoticed.

Tyron made her strip naked in front of the three men, and her stunning womanhood created an excitement in the three men and, oddly enough, for that matter, in her as well. That surprised her! As one of the men approached her, she felt she was as ready as they were. She lay back on the bed, and as she did, the man got on with her and lowered his mouth to her waiting vagina. She felt a rush of sexual passion that became uncontrollable, her whole body started to shake with pleasure, and at the last moment she had an extended orgasm. She was euphoric and responded in kind as soon as he was done. At that point, the other two men in the room approached her, and she was eager to please them as well. One of the men placed his member in her mouth, held her head, and started to move her up and down his cock as another entered her from behind. She felt heat rising once again, and as she exploded in another orgasm, the man in her mouth did as well. Tyron could see the passion in her eyes, and for the moment, he wished he could have his turn as well. One after another and at several times two at a time had sex with her as Tyron looked on. For her, it was as much a pleasure as it was humiliating; she had one orgasm after another, and that not only made her more aggressive but seemed to excite the men even more. She later would remember pushing one of the men down and getting on top of him to satisfy her as much as she wanted to satisfy him. *Totally fucked up!* she thought.

Finally, after more than two hours, they left her below deck and went above to have some drinks and some laughs with Tyron. Tears filled her eyes as she went to the stateroom bathroom to clean herself up. What she saw in the mirror helped her make a life-changing decision. It was at that time Claire decided that if she ever got back to shore, she was done with the type of life she had been living. Tyron did indeed get the yacht to the Bahamas, and after several days of the same treatment of Claire, he left the three men ashore and ordered Claire back on the boat and headed back to Florida. Claire not only felt used but also felt a hatred for Tyron that consumed her, and she made up her mind that she would get out of this affair and head back to Atwood the first chance she ha.

Tyron docked the boat on the end of the channel he lived on, smiled at Claire, and asked her if she had a great time. She was consumed with hate for the man before her, a man that, until this trip, she thought she loved. "It was great," she said, and as she did, she held out her arms as if to welcome Tyron into her embrace, thinking all the time how much she hated the whole experience and now Tyron as well. He approached her from across the room, and as he did, she undid the nightshirt she was wearing and exposed her beautiful body to him in a way he could not resist. He held her in his arms as she ripped his shirt off and unbuckled his belt and pulled down his shorts. She led him back to the state room in which she had been raped by his friends and pulled him onto that same bed. Tyron was euphoric and his erection was never harder as he thought of the pleasures he was about to receive. Claire lay back on the bed and with open legs and an alluring smile beckoned him to enter her. As he got up on his knees to accept her offerings, he closed his eyes in anticipation of the conquest and the pleasure he was about to receive.

The first thing he felt was her lips and mouth engulfing his penis. But his sigh of pleasure was cut short when he felt the pain of a butcher knife Claire had brought out from under the pillow entering his chest just below his heart. When he pulled away, he felt the knife again at his throat. His eyes bulged as he looked at her now blood-covered body, realizing that the blood was his; he could feel the life leaving his body. He tried to talk, but no words came out. His vision blurred, and Claire smiled. It was the last thing he would ever see.

Claire rolled over from under the dead arrogant asshole and pushed him on to the floor. It was now late at night, and there was nothing but silence on the dock. She calmly pulled the dead body to the side of the boat, tied the boat's extra anchor around his waist, and with a little effort pushed him over the side. She took a quick shower, dressed, and left the boat and what she thought would be this life behind forever.

CHAPTER 44

SOME THINGS NEVER CHANGE

Claire woke up and watched as Richards reattached his artificial leg. It occurred to her during the wild evening they had shared together that of all the men she had been with in all the places she had been, this was a first for her, and not too many things were a first anymore. She had never been with a man, or for that matter a woman, who had a part missing. She felt confident enough to ask him how he had lost his leg.

She rolled over and propped herself on one elbow, letting the sheets covering her slide down to her waist so he could see the upper half of her body. She wanted to weaken his ability to resist her forthcoming questions.

"Good morning, Kent. What a great night. I hope you enjoyed it as much as I did." *I actually did!* she thought.

The normally gruff Richards smiled, and it was as if his whole personality had changed. "Never in my life have I ever experienced anything like that. It was truly amazing." The charms and her body had worked its magic once again. She could tell that he would help her get rid of George. The promise she made to herself long ago to always be in charge was never more important. In a soft, practiced, sexy voice, she decided to ask about the leg.

"What, if I may ask, happened to your leg? I would have never known if we hadn't gotten naked. You may need it for other things, but last night it made no difference." Immediately, she knew she had crossed a line with him that she might not get back over. His gentle smile turned menacing. She saw the pupils become almost pinpoint. It scared her so much that she raised the sheets up to cover her breasts. He had a coffee cup in his hand as he stood and flung it across the room, smashing against a mirror above the small desk. Glass flew everywhere. Claire pulled the sheet the rest of the way to avoid being cut.

"You want to know about this leg, let me tell you. You don't have it in you to understand what this means, never, never in a thousand years would you, or for that matter anyone else, either. Sometimes I don't understand it myself."

Claire cowered behind the sheets.

"There are too many nightmares and too many deaths that have been the results of the way I lost this leg." Richards pounded on the desk with his fists, hitting it so hard the legs on the cheap hotel piece of furniture collapsed into a heap on the floor.

"I'm sorry I asked, truly I am. It's not that important," Claire said.

Richards turned and stared at her with a leer so heated it could set the room ablaze.

"Not important, not important? Let me tell you something, you stupid bitch. It's so important that if not for thinking about it all the time I would not be here in this room or in this town with you in a million years."

"I don't understand why being here in Atwood has anything to do with your missing leg," Claire offered as she drew the sheets up tighter.

The anger in his face seemed to ebb, and as it did, his voice began to take on a calmer tone. The sheer menace on his face faded and was replaced by not a smile, but the familiar smirk, which to Claire seemed like a big improvement. Richards was taking control over his emotions now because he knew he needed Claire to remain as his contact to Maples in an effort to set him up for the kill. Richards sat on the end of the bed, turned to Claire, and said, "It's too long and too complicated to tell you everything, but let me just say one thing—Hank Maples!"

CHAPTER 45

A LONG WAY FROM HOME

Richards looked again in the folder that Amed had given him, and it truly was complete. Everything he needed to get back to the States was there, and the first test of how good everything was was about to happen as he waited to board a plane that would get him to South America. The closer to home he got, although he did not consider the USA home anymore, the more uptight he had become. The distance he had to travel over the time it took was kindling a fire in him to get to Maples that he had so far been able to suppress, but as the trip neared its end, the pent-up hatred was starting to boil, and he almost lost it all when in a bar in Argentina after one or perhaps two too many drinks he had made a pass at a young women that apparently was with her boyfriend.

Once the pushing and shoving started, the owner of the small bar and several of the patrons faced off with Richards, who under normal circumstances would be a match for several men, and pushed him out the door into the dusty, trash-strewn street. As he turned to leave, one of the men followed him to the rear of the bar and egged him on to fight. Normally when that same situation occurred in the past,

Richards would have taken up the offer and more than likely would punish the aggressor. This time, though, with his eye on the prize, he declined to fight and turned to leave.

As he walked away, the man ran around and got in front of him, taunting him and yelling at him in a language he didn't understand. Richards knew the type and thought that if he continued to walk away the man would stop and return to the bar. The rest of the men from the bar yelled something to their friend, and again Richards had no clue what they were saying, but he watched them re-enter the small bar. *Too bad for this man*, Richards thought, and as he turned the corner into the darkness that an alley provided between the building and the street, he turned to face his enemy. The man was about four inches shorter that Richards but had a well-developed body. Richards thought he must be on some sort of steroids to look like he did.

The man yelled once again in the same language and with the same tone then charged at Richards with blind rage. It took Richards by surprise just how fast this man was with his fists, but the trouble was that when he missed hitting Richards, he slipped and fell to the ground, and feeling embarrassed, he jumped back up. As he did, he lunged at Richards but was stopped in his tracks as he felt a sharp pain in his side. When he looked down, there was blood pouring from a wound in his groin area. His eyes widened, and he fell to the ground, writhing in pain and once again screaming in the language Richards still didn't understand but at least now he knew what the man was trying to say.

Not wanting to delay the moment, Richards bent over and looked in the man's eyes that now seemed to beg for mercy. Richards' plane was due to take off in about an hour, and the airport was ten minutes away. True to his way of leaving no one to remember him, he spoke softly to the man on the ground, whose eyes now showed real fear, simply saying, "Goodbye." He slid the knife across the man's throat from ear to ear, and as the blood started to pump the life out of the man, Richards walked away. When he got far enough from the alley, he hailed a cab and was off to the airport. Next stop: the USA. He was getting closer to Maples and finishing the task ahead.

CHAPTER 46

FEET ON THE GROUND

merica! Richards thought as he stepped on US soil for the first time in many years. The trip from South America to the States landed him at the international airport in Miami. Crow had indeed taken care of everything, and Richards walked to the next terminal, where he would catch a plane that would take him to his new home state of West Virginia. The paperwork that Crow had arranged for had to this point worked flawlessly, and Richards had no reason to think that there would be any trouble now that he was in the States. As he sat in an airport bar drinking a Jack Daniels, he raised his glass to make a toast. In almost a whisper, Richards said, "Here's to you, Crow, for a great job!"

A man sitting next to him turned to him and asked if he was speaking to him. "No, sir, just remembering a man that was a very important part of my being here today."

"I assume that your friend is departed?" his new companion asked.

Richards stared straight ahead and snickered, "I'm afraid so." He felt some remorse for Crows demise. *Live by the sword, die by the sword,* he thought.

"Well, I'm sorry to hear that, but time marches on, and whatever life holds for you next may help you get over your past," said the man. "I can tell from your tone you are hurting. Let me buy you a drink and perhaps offer you some words from the Bible!"

"Save it, pastor. I have better things to do than listen to that shit." Richards got up and walked out of the bar. *If the pastor only knew!*

The flight from Miami to Yaeger airport outside of Charleston was short, and though Richards took a cat nap, he was energized by the thought he would finally be free to start a new life here where the odds of anyone knowing him was nonexistent. He grabbed a cab and gave him the address that was included in the folder that he got from Amed. Keys to the house were in the folder as well. Twenty-five minutes later, the cab dropped Richards off in front of a small ranch house with a single attached garage where a small Ford SUV was parked. The keys were in it, and on the seat was the title and the copy of the insurance policy.

Crow had indeed done a great job. *Too bad it had to be that way,* Richards thought, but the thought only lasted a few seconds. Richards felt great as he sat on a small couch. He put his feet up on the coffee table and had to remind himself just what this was all about. *No time to get comfortable yet.* Fatigue caught up with him, and he decided he needed to get some rest, as there was a lot of planning to do. He had a sense that his efforts to kill Maples would not be as easy as he would like. He went to bed at nine and slept soundly through the night.

In the morning, he found several guns in a hidden compartment in the back of the bedroom closet, as well as a six-inch hunting knife in its own leather sheath. Once again, he thought of Crow, who had even provided Richards some information that would lead him in the direction of a drug kingpin in Ohio who had been drawing the attention of Hank Maples and the FBI. If he could contact the drug kingpin and get involved in his dealings, it would get him closer to being in position to finish his mission to kill Maples. A quick phone call and Richards was in contact with George Bandy, who had been expecting the call. *Thank God for Crow!*

CHAPTER 47

LESSONS LEARNED

Special Agent Simone Richards set up a meeting with Hank and the rest of the task force in charge of trying to shut down the flow of drugs into Ohio, and for that matter the central part of the country as well. They had set the meeting up in the office of former Sheriff Jimmy Tate, and for all intents, the office space was theirs for as long as they needed it. A new sheriff had not yet been appointed. Tate was stilled be mourned as a hero killed in the line of duty.

Atwood town leaders were happy that federal law enforcers were on the ground and taking the lead on breaking up the drug ring that had strangled their town and killed their sheriff. The one person of influence who wanted Tate quickly replaced was George Bandy. He lobbied the town council to name Tate's deputy to the job, hopeful that he could count on him as he had Tate.

George Bandy wanted a replacement for Tate so he could continue his activities with some inside help. He had met Kent Richards, and though he felt he could trust him after he had him kill Tate, he wasn't one hundred percent sure of him, especially the way he just happened to show up. He had lobbied the town council to appoint Tate's second in command, who Bandy thought he could control as he had Tate. So far, though, that hadn't been accomplished.

The agents all looked up at the same time as Hank Maples entered the office. They did so because Lacy Anderson was with him. They weren't so sure she should be included, but the fact that her newspaper background had helped them uncover a few facts about the drug dealing in the town and surrounding area gave her leverage. And so far, she had kept her promise not to disclose any details about the shootings or investigations.

Special Agent Ritter was resentful of her, and Lacy could sense it. For her part, Lacy thought that Ritter had a thing for Hank, and though Hank showed no outward signs of it, Lacy thought perhaps he and Ritter had some past issues.

"Anderson, what are you doing here? This meeting is a strategic meeting that only people with a government clearance are allowed to attend."

Lacy started to answer, but as she did, Hank spoke up. "Listen, Simone, you know as well as I do that Lacy has at least as much information to offer as anyone else in the room, so let's just put that talk on the back burner for now and get some ground work finished so we can end this shit that's happening around here and get on with our lives!"

Ritter gave a sideways glance to the rest of her team and with a roll of her eyes said to Hank, "Well, Agent Hank Maples, for those of us that have real jobs, this is the life we live and we choose to live it by the rules."

Her remarks were meant to demean the UASIS as compared to the FBI.

"No need for name calling, Simone. We're all here for the same reason—to get the bad guys. There is more to gain through cooperation than backbiting and criticism. Let's just do our jobs, shall we?"

"Okay, Hank, but if something happens to her, it's on you, not the rest of the team, you got that?"

He nodded in approval and looked at Lacy. She was so livid her face was turning red, and under the table, she balled up her fist and raised up her middle finger and whispered to Hank, "Fuck that bitch."

Hank thought perhaps Lacy was jealous of Simone.

"To date, this is what we know for sure, at least what we think is for sure," Ritter said as she took the cover off a rather large white board that had various pictures and a timeline graph on it. Maples wondered what she meant by "at least we think." The Army and USAIS would certainly be better than that, but again he held his words and thoughts to himself.

On the board, there were open spaces where names should be as if it was an ancestry chart. As the names spread out below, many had been filled, but those at the top were empty, meaning that the task force was good at identifying the low-level runners but had failed at the top of the food chain. The names of those killed in the ambush at the cabin on Smoke Mountain Road were crossed out with red exes. It was about the top of the chart that this meeting had been convened.

"Based on the flow of drugs in this part of the country, the conclusion is that the names we need to fill the top of this chart must be people with close ties to this location and must have connections close by as well," Ritter said. She then turned over to the next page, and on it was a list of names considered to be suspects, some of which startled Lacy and Hank.

The list was written in red, and there were more than ten names on it. Hank looked at Lacy and then again at the white board in disbelief. One of the names was George Bandy. Lacy stood, approached Ritter, and said, "How in the world did this list of names come to be? I have known George Bandy most of my life. I cannot imagine him mixed up in any of the things going on here and even more so that he would have a reach beyond Atwood. No way in hell!"

"Back off, Ms. Anderson, and please return to your seat. You're out of your depth here and are better off listening than running your mouth!" Ritter admonished.

Lacy returned to her chair beside Hank, who was also shaken to see George's name there. Hank had known George as a youth and always saw him as accomplished and upstanding. However, Mrs. Bandy's relationship with Sheriff Tate had been troubling him, and he wondered if it was Bandy who he saw the night of the raid fleeing in the car that sped off. *Keep an open mind,* he told himself.

"What the fuck, Hank? How can that be true?" asked Lacy, who again challenged Special Agent Ritter.

"Agent Ritter, as I said, I have known George Bandy my entire life, and you have to be wrong. What makes you think he could possibly have anything to do with this? As you know, I have been doing research for my newspaper on this, and I have found nothing implicating George."

Ritter took a step toward Lacy but then backed off. "First, Ms. Anderson, for the last time, please refer to me as *Special* Agent. Secondly, it is apparent to me that your investigating skills may need some refining. Thirdly, if you cannot abide by the rules that I set that allow you join these meetings with Agent Maples, please use the door at the back and let yourself out."

Lacy stood and turned her back to Ritter, looked at Hank, and huffed, "I'll see you later." As she turned to leave, she said, "Fuck you, *Agent* Ritter."

All Hank could do was think, *Whew!* But he wondered what actions Lacy would take by herself.

Ritter composed herself and then looked directly at Hank and said, "Listen, Hank, it wasn't very smart of me to allow Ms. Anderson's involvement in our efforts here. I did that as a favor to you. Consider the favor over, and if and when you see her, please let her know what I said I meant, no second chances. We cannot have our team compromised in any way, you got that?" Hank responded that he did. "Good, end of subject," Ritter replied.

"Now let's get back to the business at hand, if you all don't mind." Ritter went on to explain that when the ambush at Smoke Mountain went down, the other federal agents had high-definition cameras in place and pictures of several men who managed to escape and that some had now been identified by face and name, and others were only faces with no names. George Bandy was among those identified.

So, it was Bandy in the car, Hank thought.

Ritter turned another page, and the face on it was that of someone Hank recognized instantly, but the name didn't match. The ghost that he'd mentioned to Lacy was apparently alive. He stared in almost disbelief when he stood and looked at Ritter.

"What is it now, Maples?" Ritter asked.

"I don't know how it's possible, but the man in that picture is not Kent Richards. He's a US Army deserter, a drug dealer who I thought I had killed in Vietnam years ago. His name is Ronald Evers. I just cannot believe it."

Bandy was with Evers. Why? Hank thought. *What the fuck is going on here?*

"I'm not sure what you mean by that, Agent Maples," Ritter said. "This man has been positively identified as indicated. He's an Army vet honorably discharged, a businessman from Charleston, West Virginia, and apparently a syndicate drug dealer."

"He very well may be a drug dealer, but I guarantee you that the man in that picture is Ronald Evers. Look up his bio in the USAIS portfolio. He deserted his post in Vietnam and was running drugs and everything else illegal for many years until we had him cornered. I nearly blew his leg off. If this man, Kent Richards, is who I think it is, he is either missing a leg or has one that is severely scarred."

Hank related to the group all he knew that had happened, and when he was done, Ritter told him she would check out the story. Meanwhile, the task force would forge ahead with a plan to put an end to George Bandy and Kent Richards or whoever the mystery man turned out to be. Plans were made to follow Bandy for the next several days or even weeks until he could be trapped and brought to justice. Hank, on the other hand, knew he had to take matters into his own hands if he expected to live much longer. Evers, he thought, was in Atwood for reasons other than running drugs. Hank knew his life was in danger, and to survive, he would have to be smarter and even more aggressive than Evers.

CHAPTER 48

BEGINNING OF THE END

When Maples left the meeting, he found Lacy sitting on a bench outside the sheriff's office where the meeting had been held. He could tell by the look on her face that she was pissed, and when he went to her and sat down beside her, she jumped up and pointed a finger that all but poked out his eye she was so close. "What else did that fucking bitch in there have to say about me?" Lacy asked, and the tone of her voice indicated she wanted a straight answer, not some bullshit.

"So here's the thing. From now on, you aren't allowed to be involved in any way in the investigation. You won't be able to have any information gathered by the task force either for your story or for anything else as well," Hank said

Lacy's face flushed with rage. "She cannot do that, god damn it! And you of all people shouldn't let her stick it to me. I think she has the hots for you and thinks with me out of the way she can have you all for herself, that bitch!"

"Calm down, Lacy. Let's not go overboard with crazy talk. I'm sure we can work something out, and if not then, we will look for other ways to keep you involved."

"You know what, Hank? Fuck all that. I'll continue to work on the story by myself. I wouldn't want you to jeopardize your position or your mission. If you can't or won't help me, then I will do it anyway I can, and as of now, that means you should find another place to stay. Your welcome at my place just wore out!"

With that, Lacy turned and started to walk to the car they had come in to meet with the task force. "And when I say get another place, I mean by the end of the day!"

Hank watched her walk away, and as he did, Special Agent Ritter walked up to him with a smile on her face that made him feel that what Lacey had said just might be true. *Shit!* "My, my, my," said Ritter. "I hope it wasn't something I said that got her all pissed off like that." When Hank turned to look at her, he could see a slight smile on her face and a gleam in her eyes that made him think that what Lacy had said about Ritter having the hots for him might just be true, but that only spelled more trouble for him if it was. He knew he would have a hard time convincing Lacy that he did care about her and this would make it harder.

He needed to try and not only ignore Simone, but to stay away from her as well. After all, she was quite attractive in a very sexy. Now that Lacy was out of the picture, Hank feared he could be easily swayed. Better to remove the temptation.

"I think it best if we both work this case together but separately," he said. "I will keep my contacts with USAIS, and you and the rest of the FBI team work from your side and we can cover more ground that way, share information with each other, and work out a final plan to get this case finished."

"Sounds good to me," Ritter said, obviously insulted and hurt. "Why not have our first meeting right now and establish some ground rules so we won't be duplicating efforts? How about dinner and a drink at Delany's? I'll meet you there with my team in fifteen minutes."

Reluctantly, Hank agreed, but he said he would need more time as he had to go to Lacy's and get the few belongings he had there.

"I have an errand that needs to be attended to. I will meet you there at seven tonight."

Ritter gave him a thumb up and got into the black standard-issue SUV the feds used.

CHAPTER 49

ONE DOWN TWO TO GO

Lacy didn't realize what George Bandy was capable of, and that led her to his doorstep. In her fury, she decided to confront George. After ringing the bell and stepping back as the door opened, she had no idea what was going to transpire, but she had made a commitment to herself to outwit both the FBI and Hank Maples as well.

Lacy was quite surprised when Claire Bandy opened the door.

"Lacy, what a nice surprise! We were just talking about you and the story we hear you're working on. Come right in."

Lacy watched as George came in from the kitchen. Based on the aroma of bacon cooking, he must have been making lunch. George walked over to Lacy and put his arms around her.

"Great to see you, Lacy. Not sure why you are here, but please join us for brunch. Nothing I like better than having an early afternoon meal with friends."

Lacy thought that when she confronted George with the accusations, it would either enrage him if he was guilty or baffle him if the opposite. At this point, she was confused and had no opinion as to which the answer might be. She entered the house, and as she looked around at the furnishings and the decorations, she wondered how a simple man could afford all she saw. Claire, of course, was dressed to the hilt even though it was mid-morning. Lacy thought that George must have had a lot to offer to land a wife that looked as great as Claire did. For a moment, she wondered what it would be like to look like that. It would seem to her that the world would be hers for the taking.

"Thanks, Mr. Bandy, but I really can't stay. I just wanted to ask you a few questions about the story I'm working on."

"I know you are writing about the drugs in our area, and though I am aware of it, I'm not sure how I can be of help," George offered and then motioned for her to come into the kitchen. "Please follow me into the kitchen while I finish fixing our brunch. Again, feel free to join Claire and me. It's not every day we get a chance to share."

"Well, thanks again, but I really have another place I need to be very shortly. If you would rather, I can come back another time that would be more convenient."

"It's no problem, Lacy. It won't take much time to find out that I know nothing about any of the mess around here, so ask away."

Claire walked over to the bar and poured flutes of champagne for her and George. She nodded to Lacy and asked if she would at least have a drink with them. Lacy decided that she might just need a bit of liquid courage to ask George the pointed questions she hoped to get answers to.

"That would be great, Claire, but just a small one will do."

"Wonderful. Never too early for bubbly," Claire said as she poured Lacy a flute almost to the top.

George stepped to the stove, took a long sip of the drink, and stirred whatever was in the pan on the stove. Lacy steadied herself and asked George a loaded question.

"Mr. Bandy, I was just kicked out of a meeting that took place regarding what's happening around here. And as much as I don't believe it, your name came up as someone being involved."

George looked at Lacy out of the corner of his eye and then looked at Claire. He steadied himself.

"And just what would anyone have a question about concerning me?" George asked.

"Well, as much as I hate to tell you, there are people here from the government, in fact two agencies, the FBI and another one associated with the Army, USAIS, that seem to think you are involved with the illegal drugs that are coming into Ohio, and they are trying to link you to the movement of them. They even have a picture of you and someone named Kent Richards, who they say works for you, or perhaps with you."

"First, Lacy, let me just say that you have known me a long time. Secondly, why is it that you would have been in a meeting with the feds and whoever else is involved? You're a newspaper reporter," Bandy asked, and as he did, he stole a look at Claire, who showed a small glimmer of fear on her otherwise flawless face.

"Yes, I am doing an investigative research about the drug problem we have in Atwood, the county, and this entire region. I have been working on it for months. When Ralph died, I saw Hank Maples at the funeral, and we started seeing each other. You may not know this, but Hank and I dated back in high school. We lost touch after he went to fight in Vietnam. Hadn't seen him since."

"What is it that Hank does, exactly?" George asked.

"He is with agency called USAIS that finds and arrest Army deserters. He came to this area on assignment and then got involved in the drug investigation that, between us, the feds think Jimmy Tate was somehow involved in."

Lacy looked at Claire to see her reaction to the mention of Tate. She gulped her champagne and poured another.

The feds are getting close, too close, Claire thought. *If they take George down, they'll probably come after me, too.* More than ever, she needed Kent Richards to solve her problem. And she needed to find out as much as she could from Lacy without seeming it to be too obvious, or for that matter raising suspicion in George, either.

"I'm sorry if I am rambling on, Mr. Bandy, but this whole thing has me both excited and confused as well."

"That's okay, Lacy. Just slow down a bit and tell me again why you would be at the meeting and anything else you might be thinking," George said.

Lacy went on to explain to George, and Claire as well, how she came to be involved with Hank Maples and then Maples getting involved with the FBI in a joint effort to put a lethal end to the drug activity in the state and in particular in the Atwood area. She also told them how Hank was looking for a man named Ronald Evers that somehow was now being called Kent Richards. She was out of control and didn't realize that she was telling them more than they should know, considering the feds thought of them as suspects. When she was through and looked at them through a reporter's eye, she realized then that she just may have fucked up! "Well, I'm sure none of this is true. I'll keep doing some research on this, and I'm sure I will be able to find the truth. I think there may still be some clues at the cabin where Sheriff Tate was killed." She hoped they believed her as she turned to the door to leave.

She had her doubts now that she had watched their eyes as she rambled on. Perhaps, she thought, Ritter was right after all. George turned from his cooking and gripped Lacy's arm as he escorted her to the door. He said in a firm but commanding way, "Don't worry, Lacy. All will end up just fine, and in the end, you will get what you deserve!" As the door closed behind her, she wondered what George thought she deserved. *Did he just threaten me?*

Claire went to the window and watched as Lacy drove off. She heard George pick up the phone and dial a number from the auto dial system. When the voice on the other end answered, George simply said, "We need to meet. We have a problem, and that problem is heading to the old cabin. It needs taken care of now!"

CHAPTER 50

STAYING IN
THE GAME

Hank thought he better get to Lacy's house as fast as he could after she left him sitting there on the bench outside the sheriff's office and gave him orders to get his shit out and fast. When he opened the door to Lacy's house, she wasn't home, but his belongings were piled on top of the couch; what wasn't in plastic garbage bags was casually tossed on top where there was a note attached to his favorite shirt. He noticed that there was a slice in the breast area where the logo of the company that made the shirt used to be. He didn't remember for sure but thought it wasn't there the last time he wore it. *Damn*, he thought, *she really was mad!*

As he took out the last of three loads, he spotted her car in front of Claire and George Bandy's house, and at the same time, he saw Lacy exit the house, get into her car, and quickly drive off in the direction out of town. Not knowing where she was headed and realizing she might still be mad, he decided to keep his distance but still try and keep her in his sight.

When Lacy left the Bandy house, she thought about the shootout on Smoke Mountain Road and thought if she went back there she might find some clues somehow that would either prove George Bandy was part of the problem or part of the solution that would at least shed light on who was involved. She had no idea what she was looking for, but because the Bitch Special Agent Ritter saying something about HD cameras posted there, she would at least go and wander around the old cabin where Tate had been killed.

Lacy drove cautiously and from time to time looked in her rearview mirror to see if she was being followed. She couldn't believe it when she thought she saw that idiot Hank in his truck about half mile behind her. She had said her piece, and she meant it, and now the asshole was following her. She needed to put a stop to that. She was and wanted to work alone now that all the shit had hit the fan. She sped up, and once around a curve in the road, she pulled off to the side and went down a small incline so he would not see her when he went by where she had turned off. When Hank sped by the curve, he continued on without seeing her car.

Hank cursed as he rounded the curve, realizing she had eluded him. After another five miles further down the road, he knew he'd lost her but was unsure how that had happened. He knew the roads out here but also knew that Lacy probably knew them better and had turned off on some hidden lane that was undetectable from the road. He decided to stop and turn around, go slower, and try to find where she had ditched him. If he couldn't, he would just return to town and meet up with Ritter and the rest of the team. She'd wanted to meet at Delany's at seven p.m. It was almost seven now, and if there was to be any peace at the meeting, he didn't want to be late. Ritter was very good at her job, but at the same time, she could be a real bitch if things did not go her way. He had seen that and wanted no more of her scorn.

Lacy watched as she saw Hank and his fancy truck head back in the direction of Atwood. Now she thought she could continue her little trip to the cabin and have some peace and quiet as she searched for clues. She may have seen Maples and thought she outfoxed him, but at the same time, she failed to see the real threat. She continued on, and about fifteen minutes later, she had arrived at the old cabin where she hoped to find something that would prove George was either innocent or, hopefully not, guilty. Still not sure what she was looking for, she got out of the car and headed to the cabin. She thought she might know it when she saw it.

Kent Richards had returned to the scene as well and was hiding in the distance when Lacy pulled up. After his chat with George Bandy, Richards headed straight to the old cabin. The phone call he had gotten from Bandy left nothing to the imagination; Lacy Anderson would have to be eliminated.

Lacy looked around the cabin and then went outside looking for anything that might give her a bit of information. She decided the trip was a waste of time, so she went back to her car and headed down the gravel road back towards town.

What a jerk I am, she thought. *Who do you think you are, Lacy, Sherlock Holmes?*

Lacy decided to find Hank and try and apologize for her hasty decision and maybe make amends with him and see if he would somehow work with her again. As she left the cabin, she didn't see Richards watching her go. If she did, she might have wondered why he was smiling from ear to ear. Lacy sped down the winding road that led back to town. It was still early enough that if she could find Hank and apologize to him, he might just move back in! What she didn't see was the trail of liquid leaking from under her car. But she would never know!

CHAPTER 51

THREE JACKS AND A QUEEN

Hank arrived at Delany's almost on time, and when he looked around for Special Agent Ritter and her team, he was surprised to see that she was the only one there. Well, maybe he wasn't, if the truth be known.

"Evening, Hank, glad you showed up," Ritter said. She had watched him enter Delany's and look around for the team but also saw the look on his face when he noticed that she was alone. She wasn't sure if she saw him smile as she had hoped he would or twist his lips in a smirk.

Hank sat down across from Simone, and as he did the waitress approached and offered to take his drink order. He looked at Simone and noticed she had a glass of wine and realized that this was not exactly going to be the planning meeting he thought it was going to be, so he ordered a Jack Daniels on the rocks. "I thought this was going to be a meeting with the entire team. What happened to them?"

"Truth is, Hank, I told them to take some time to themselves. They have been working round the clock and needed to rest their minds. You and I, on the other hand, have some things that need discussed."

The waitress had dropped off Hank's drink, Ritter raised her glass, and the two clinked their glasses. Thinking that Lacy had just thrown him out and at least for now was not in the picture, Hank looked at Simone in a different way.

"You know, Hank, we really did get off on the wrong foot. I was anxious to get to know you. We've worked with your agency before, and as a joint task force combined, we have done some real good work. As much as I hate to admit it, I may have been a bit envious of the relationship you seemed to have had with Ms. Anderson. Sorry if I caused a disruption in the romance."

"No need to feel that way, Simone. We were just friends anyway, and you might as well know she asked me to get out of her house. I was just staying in the spare room while we worked this case together."

With a wink, Ritter raised her wine glass and looked Hank in the eyes.

"So, Simone, what do we do now that you think George Bandy is the head of this gang and the man you say is Kent Richards is his partner, the man who I am telling you is Ronald Evers?" The waitress stopped by to take a food order, and Hank and Simone decided to split a pizza and order another drink. This wasn't the evening that Hank anticipated, but at the same time, it was heading in a direction he might enjoy.

Ritter never bothered to answer Hank's question about what the next step was going to be in the task to round up the bad guys. Her talk and her manner softened and became increasingly flirtatious. Hank thought it might be the wine or the fact that he'd let her know about the big break up with Lacy. Maybe Lacy was right to be jealous.

The pizza arrived, and so did the drinks, and as they shared the food and casual talk, Hank began to feel the whiskey's effects.

"So how is it that a brilliant and stunning-looking woman like you ended up with the FBI and alone and apparently single?"

"Relationships always seem to evade me as I travel around the country chasing bad guys, so I just find it easier to be casual about all that. Oh, by the way, thanks."

"Thanks for what?" Hank asked, and as he did, Simone put her hand on his.

"The stunning part. And just so you know, I can be that in more ways than one!"

Hank knew that he was in deeper than he planned but was enjoying the sinking feeling he was getting. In fact, he was silently telling himself that this indeed was going to be a special night after all.

With the pizza done and the bill paid, Hank started to stand and tell Simone good night, but as he did, he sort of wobbled a bit. He knew then he didn't really need the third Jack Daniels.

"Whoa there, Mr. Maples. Looks like you need to ask for a ride home. Doesn't look like you're in any shape to drive."

Hank had been worse at times and still could drive, or at least thought he could, but he also remembered he had no place to go for the night.

"Guess I should be going," he said.

"Going where?" Ritter asked. "Thought you got kicked out of Lacy's. Why don't you stay with me tonight?"

"Well, if you really don't mind, I just might take you upon that."

Simone led Hank out the door of Delany's, locked her arm in his, and escorted him to her SUV. She opened the passenger door for him, kissed him full on the lips, pushed him into the vehicle, and closed the door. Simone walked around the back of the car and headed for her hotel room.

Hank's mind started to sober up a bit, and he was excited for the rest of the night to play out.

Hank stirred from a deep sleep when he heard a phone beep. As he sat up in bed, the first thing that came to his mind was to wonder just where the hell he was. Then he remembered that after leaving Delany's with Simone, they had driven to her hotel. He looked at the other side of the bed. Simone wasn't there, but he could hear her talking on the phone in the other room.

He wasn't sure what hotel they were in, but it was a very large double room with a small kitchen. *Nothing too good for the government,* he thought as he got up and went to the bathroom, where his clothes were hanging on a hook behind the door. Having left all his clothing and sundries he removed from Lacy's in his truck, all he could do to make some sort of effort to clean himself up was to splash some water on his face and gargle with the mouthwash provided to the guests. He would have to find a place to stay. He had no intentions to get involved with Ritter as he had with Lacy, although from what he remembered about the night before, it was very exciting. He couldn't stop thinking that Special Agent Simone Ritter was special in more ways than one.

He walked out of the bedroom and into the small but well-appointed living area and found Simone. He tried to ignore her conversation on the phone. She must have been up for a while because she was fully dressed and looked as if she had just stepped out of the pages of some fashion magazine, though in more appropriate business attire fitting a special agent, who Hank now knew as a very special agent with talents he was sure they didn't teach in FBI school. His smile was replaced on his face as he watched Simone's reaction to whatever information she was getting on her phone. The expression on her face was changing to a dour look the longer she was on the phone, and Hank could tell something was terribly wrong. As the conversation continued, she looked at Hank, and in her eyes, he could see that whatever it was concerned her and, he had a feeling, himself as well.

Simone clicked her phone off and approached Hank with a very troubled look on her face. It was not the way he expected the day to start after the night they had together.

"Hank, I have some bad news. Perhaps you might want to have a seat before I tell you about the phone call I just had from one of my team members."

Hank never thought it would be anything that would concern him, so he was a bit surprised by her insinuation for him to have a seat. When she said, "Lacy Anderson is dead," he all but crumbled to the floor and indeed took a seat on the couch in the living room. Hank tried to open his mouth to ask what happened, and the words just wouldn't come out.

He was stunned to a point that he could barely breathe, and he felt his heart racing at what must have been an unhealthy pace. His mind raced as well, and his vision blurred to a point that he felt so lightheaded that he thought he'd pass out. Simone saw the reaction in his body movements and hurried to his side on the couch. She put her strong arms around his shoulders and gave him a reassuring hug. His head fell to her chest, and she cradled him in her arms as a mother would a child in distress. It seemed like minutes, but in reality, it was only a few seconds. Hank pushed away and asked Simone what had happened and if she was sure of what she was saying.

"What happened? What do we know?" Hank asked.

"That was agent Lombardo on the phone. He got a call from a deputy at the Atwood Sheriff's Department regarding a fatal traffic accident out on the highway near Smoke Mountain Road. He called us because he knew Lacy had been working with us and thought we needed to know. I'm so sorry."

Ritter made coffee, poured Hank a cup, and set it in front of him, hoping he would drink some and settle down.

"We need to get out there and inspect the scene," he said. "And where is Lacy now? I have to do something. I just can't sit here and do nothing."

"I know it's easy for me to say, but try and relax and calm down. We will go out there and see if we can find out what happened," Ritter offered, and with that, Hank picked up the cup of coffee in front of him and took a long pull on the refreshing liquid.

Ritter and Hank arrived on scene while the wrecking crew was attempting to extract the wreckage from the bottom of a drop-off on the road at a curve. They could see the guard rail had been run through, and the car had landed about one hundred feet down into the rocks and the river below. Hank could see the crew down there, and he started to climb down, thinking Lacy was still there; he needed to see her for himself in order to have some closure. The sheriff's deputy on scene as well as Agent Lombardo told him that Lacy's body had been removed and the effort was underway to get the car back up from the riverbed below; there was nothing he could do but try to relax, and they would let him know if they found anything that would help in determining what had happened. They expected that speed was the causing factor. They guessed she was speeding at this point in the road and simply lost control, tragic but just that.

Hank wouldn't be denied, though, and he started to climb down the side of the steep ravine. After telling him to hold up, Ritter gave up and followed him down the incline. The crew down by the riverbed was trying to figure out a way to hook up lines that would allow them to get Lacy's car back up on the road. As it sat, it was upside down and resting in about two feet of water. By the time Hank and Ritter got down to the riverbed, the crew had secured several lines to the demolished car. Hank had been in that same car with Lacy on a number of occasions, and if he did not know it was hers, it would be unrecognizable. It was no wonder she didn't survive, he thought as a tear dropped from his eye, and as it did, he remembered he now had shed tears twice here in Atwood.

The wrecking crew started to give a signal to the truck operator up on the road to start the pulley and get the car on up the embankment, but Hank yelled over to one of them to ask if he could have a few minutes to survey the wreckage before it went back up. It made no difference to them, they said; they worked by the hour, and the more time it took, the better for them! The car being upside down allowed Hank and Simone to view the wreckage from an odd perspective, which let Hank look inside for clues of some sort. Perhaps Lacy had been drinking because of the breakup and the fight they had gotten into yesterday. If so, he would never forgive himself, though it was her temper that started the tiff.

Realizing that there wasn't much chance of getting inside until the car was hoisted up the embankment and then turned back over, Maples and Ritter looked over the bottom of the car to see if there had been a malfunction of some sort that was plain to see. Hank wondered if Lacy had a flat tire or something of that nature; perhaps a steering linkage had broken or some other mechanical failure of some sort. Not being a mechanic but having worked on cars when he was a teen, Hank had a small amount of knowledge of how cars worked and at times why they didn't. When he was checking the front tire for damage, he all but froze in his tracks. He turned to Ritter, who was behind the rear of the car and said, "What the fucking hell is this shit? The brake line has been cut. Someone wanted to make sure Lacy ended up dead. She must have been on to something, and they had to get rid of her!"

From his vantage point across the small ravine and up the other side of the riverbank, Ronald Evers was watching with a glare in his eyes. He was getting close to the end of the hunt, and he could all but smell the blood of his final victim, Hank Maples. He was as close to getting his revenge as he had ever been. As he thought about his quest for revenge, he wondered if he had gone overboard in his attempt to find and kill Maples.

As he watched Maples climb out of the ravine, he thought that maybe some of the people that had gotten in his way may not have had to die. Then as Maples cleared the top with Special Agent Ritter, he felt the phantom pain in his artificial leg and dismissed the soft thoughts he just had. He knew deep down that those he had killed were just steps on the ladder he needed to take to finally end his sworn promise he made to himself some years back. He would have to wait a bit now that others were involved, but he would prevail in the end; he was sure of that. He realized that because of Claire, he would have access to even more money if she came through with the betrayal of her loving husband. *Yep,* he thought, *George will have to go, and then Maples will be the last.* The thought that he would also be rid of Kent Richards brought a smile to his face. For better or worse, he would be Ronald Evers again.

CHAPTER 52

CAN'T BRING BACK YESTERDAY

Hank grabbed Ritter by the arm and pulled her aside as they both got to the top of the hillside. Out of earshot of the others, he said, "I didn't believe you yesterday, and neither did Lacy, and it got her killed. I think I know who did this, but we need to work together to prove it. I think George Bandy is, indeed, the prick you guys say he is and is responsible for Lacy's death."

Ritter turned to face him with a bit of a smile and asked why the change of heart.

"After the argument yesterday between Lacy and me, she asked me to get out of her house. When I went there after the meeting, she wasn't home, but I saw her car parked in the driveway of George Bandy's house. I bet she went there to ask him about the insinuations she heard at the meeting. No telling what he thought of that. I guess at that point in time I was reluctant to believe it myself. I think he listened, and then when he realized that Lacy and the rest of the team were getting close to catching him, he must have had her killed. I think that crazy fucker Kent Richards, who is actually Ronald Evers, either cut the brake line on her car or got someone else to do it. George wouldn't have the balls to do it himself. I even tried to follow her when she left Bandy's house, but I lost track of her. She must have seen me in her rearview mirror and ditched me."

When Maples was done ranting, Special Agent Simone Ritter leaned against the now right side up car and stroked her beautiful chin and pulled at her hair, which gave Maples a rush as he remembered scenes from last night.

"So just what do you think we should do, Maples?"

"I'm not sure, but the quicker we do something, the better off everyone will be," he responded and then added, "I think your team is better equipped to deal with this the rest of the way, so how about you tell me what we need to do and I will give you one hundred percent of my time and any other help I can get from USAIS? Just keep me in the loop."

Ritter smiled, but not too brightly as she didn't want Hank to get the impression she thought she was better at this game than him, but in her heart she knew she was.

"Here is another thing we need to be concerned with as well as trying to catch them in the commission of a crime. We need to protect you as well," Ritter said.

Hank glared at her. "Fuck you, Special Agent Ritter. I can take care of myself. I don't need you or the FBI to babysit me, you understand?"

Ritter smiled and looked straight into Hank's eyes and with a bit of a sparkle said, "First, yes you can fuck me, and second I'm not sure you can take care of yourself if the result is anything like how Ms. Anderson was taken care of. We have a killer on the loose, and you may be in his sights."

Hank was furious, and as soon as Ritter mentioned Lacy, she regretted it. She started to offer an apology when Hank lunged at her and swung with all his might a right hook that if it had hit Ritter it would have done some real damage. As it was, the fist missed her by about a foot when she dodged to her left and then as quickly as she did, she seemed to spring back to her right and clipped Hank on his left temple. It stunned him not only with the pain, which dropped him to his knees, but also just how fast she was and how powerful her strength seemed to be. Another thing she must have learned in FBI school!

"You see, Hank, that's another thing you need to learn if we are going to be partners. I am the boss, and what I say goes, unless you have a better solution. Now, I am sorry about Lacy, and I shouldn't have said what I did. But if we are going to beat that bastard Bandy and his sidekick, Richards or Evers, or whoever the hell he is, then we need to be a better team. What say you?"

As he started to get up from the ground, a smile crossed his face, and as he regained his footing, he said "You're right, Simone. I guess I do need all the help I can get. Your place or mine?" He already knew the answer because he had no place of his own to go.

CHAPTER 53

THE THREAT

Lacy's funeral was put together rather quickly by her grieving parents and a few friends. Most of those in attendance were relatives. From the number of well-wishers there, it was apparent to Hank that Lacy did not have many friends. Her mother and father stood at the coffin and several other cousins or whoever they were helped Lacy's mother and father get through the day. Hank sat off to the side, as he did not want to be a distraction. To most, he was a stranger. He couldn't help but think that he should have been there for her on the day she died, but he also felt he had not been responsible for her death. He just hoped he could continue to think that way.

Special Agent Ritter sat a few rows behind him, and the rest of her team was there as well to show their respects. Hank was stunned when he watched George and Claire Bandy enter the funeral home and joined the line of well-wishers. Hank was convinced that in some way George was at least partially responsible for the death of Lacy.

Though local law enforcement had ruled the crash an accident after very little actual investigation, Hank knew the truth about the brake line, and he also knew that soon the investigators from the sheriff's office would take a better look at the ruined car, and with the help of himself and perhaps Ritter, they would see that the accident was anything but.

George and Claire approached Lacy's mother and father and in quiet tones said, "Sorry for your loss. Lacy was a fine young woman and a very good neighbor. We always watched out for each other."

It was all Hank could do to keep himself from getting up and attacking George. He made up his mind then and there that he would even the score for Lacy with Bandy and, for that matter, Claire as well if he found out she was involved in Lacy's murder. George approached Hank, who stood to confront him. George offered a handshake, and Hank refused. Unfazed by the rejection, George looked Hank in the eye.

"I know how much you thought of Lacy. I know you two were seeing each other, and the last time I talked to her, she had great things to say about you, Hank. Claire and I are very sorry for your loss."

Hank looked at them both and without a word turned and looked at Ritter as if to ignore the offered condolence from Bandy and Claire as well. Hank turned back around to face Bandy, lowered his eyes to the floor, took a step toward the couple, and leaned close to George's ear.

"This is not over, Bandy. I know what you did or, as the coward you are, had done. I am coming for you, and if I discover Claire was involved, her as well."

George and Claire left the funeral home. Having heard what Hank told him, he knew it was time to get away, and he needed Richards to help him. What he did not know was that Richards had a plan of his own, and while Claire was part of it, George was not.

"I have to make a call, honey. Why don't you go home and wait for me and we'll make plans to get dinner and some drinks downtown or at the club? I have some business to take care of that may take a while. I'll catch a ride and meet you later."

Like a good wife Claire got in the car and waved goodbye to her loving husband, thinking that it might just be the last time!

Bandy walked to his downtown office, and once inside, he opened the liquor cabinet and poured himself a glass of Scotch. He sat at his oak desk, opened a humidor that contained some rather expensive cigars, lit one up, and after taking a few long pulls and exhaling the smooth aroma decided to take some time to relax before calling Richards. When he called the number about an hour later, Richards saw George's number on caller ID and picked up after several rings. He did not want George to think he was at his beck and call or anxious to talk, though in truth he was.

"Hey, Bandy, what's up?" was what bandy heard when the call was answered. He thought to himself what an asshole Richards was and how he would be glad when this whole thing was over. He had regretted getting involved with Richards in the first place but realized he needed him now more than ever.

In the back of his mind, he regretted as well the way things had gone with Sheriff Tate. He had little trust in Richards and had wished Tate had not been such an ass and was still around to do the dirty work that Bandy needed done.

"Richards, we need to meet. Something has come up that needs your attention."

"What the fuck kind of jam are you in now?"

"I prefer not to talk about it on the phone. Let's meet in my downtown office where we'll have some privacy."

"I'll meet you there, but I'm going to need about an hour or so. Does that work for you?"

"Sure, that's great. Take your time."

Bandy hung up and went back to his drink and cigar. He relished the idea that he would now have more time to finish a great smoke, and for that matter have another drink, or maybe two.

Richards ended the call on his cell and snickered. Claire had driven to his hotel room rather than home and was waiting naked for Richards by the bed.

CHAPTER 54

THE SET UP

Claire looked across the room and watched as Richards reattached his leg. Though she had been with more men than she could count, she was in awe of the way he was able to satisfy her rather demanding needs. When he was dressed, he sat on the end of the bed, and while Claire was still flushed, he needed to be sure they were on the same page when it came to the next phase with George.

"Do you have the gold from its hiding place, Claire?" he asked her. Claire was hesitant to answer truthfully because she still had no real reason to trust Richards entirely. Claire had been privy to all of George's illegal activity, and when he had plenty of cash, he converted it to gold for two reasons. One was so there would be very little or no way the money could be traced. Secondly, he knew that no matter what happened in the world and where he might want to go, gold was the true international currency and could easily be converted into cash almost anywhere.

George's needs were modest, but his unfaithful wife's were not. She had become a liability and would continue to be. George considered paying Richards to eliminate Claire the way he had that pesky reporter. But, despite her disloyalty and extravagance, George had deep feelings for his trophy wife and was captivated by her beauty. No woman could replace her. He would give the situation more thought, but he'd have to decide his wife's future quickly as law enforcers were closing in.

"I do have it relocated to the office downtown; it is up in the finished attic," Claire told Richards. "George never goes up there because of the steep stairway. George has been away from that old building for a while, and small bunch by small bunch I was able to hide it there. He has no idea."

Richards grinned. "You really are devious," he teased. *My kind of girl,* he thought.

"I'm not sure I can go through with it, Kent. I'm afraid of getting caught, and if I do, George will have me killed. You know what he is capable of."

"I don't see where you have much choice anymore, Claire. George knows you were cheating on him and may already be taking some action to deal with that. I think you need to go on the offensive."

"I suppose you're right. It's going to come down to me or him. I understand, Kent, and I promise that by this time tomorrow, I will be ready to go."

"Sounds good to me. Perhaps you can do something about it today. I am meeting with him at the office downtown later today, and you will have a chance to make plans to move out now. Give me a call when you get all set. I will keep him busy until I hear from you."

Richards opened the front door to the old home that had served as an office building for George Bandy. It was a fully restored, turn-of-the-century home that would qualify for the National Register of Historic Buildings if it wasn't on it already. Richards had been there before but had never paid attention to the stairs off the entryway that must lead up to the attic. He would be up there soon enough.

He headed back to where he thought Bandy would be, and sure enough, when Richards opened the door to the inner office, George was there. Cigar smoke filled the room, and as Richards scanned the room, he could see that a bottle of premium single malt scotch had a big dent in it and George was enjoying the company of a young girl even younger than Claire.

"What the fuck, Richards? I expected a call when you were on your way, or at least a knock on the door before you just take the liberty of barging in here unannounced."

Bandy stood, and a young half naked woman sprang from his lap and made a quick grab for the clothes on the floor. George was fumbling clumsily trying to zip up his pants and at the same time telling the sweet young thing that she should leave by the side door. Richards tried not to laugh at the embarrassing situation that Bandy had found himself in, but he couldn't hold back and was almost bending over laughing as the young women turned and faced George as she was about to close the side door. "I still expect my money," she said as she left. "I'll collect next week when we meet again. Same time and place."

Maybe not, Richards thought. *There might not be a next week for old George.*

The door pretty much hit her bare ass as she made her hasty exit. Richards knew that there would not be a next week for that young tease, at least not with Bandy. If Richards needed proof of why Claire was fed up with George, he needed it no more. He decided right then that he and Claire would take George Bandy for all they could. Richards was certain that George had enough cash stashed that, even after he and Claire absconded with the gold, George would have enough wealth to continue his cheap whores and fat cigars. That was if Richards let him live.

Once George zipped up and regained his composure, he pointed to a chair across from the oak desk and asked Richards to have a seat. Richards sat, and Bandy pulled a glass from a drawer and poured Richards a stiff drink. He knew they had much to discuss. Without so much as a mention of what had just happened, Bandy got right to the point.

"That fucking Hank Maples confronted me today at the funeral for that Anderson bitch, and he is determined to put my ass in jail or worse. We need to stop him and that Special Agent Ritter as well if she gets in the way. There will be an extra bonus for you when the job is done. What would you say to an extra twenty thousand dollars for him and if you have to off the FBI bitch another ten?"

Richards acted grateful as he calculated the difference between what George was offering and the amount of money Claire and he would steal. *No contest,* Richards thought, *not when you toss beautiful and sexy Claire into the mix.*

Richards acted like he was contemplating the offer and took an extra few moments before he stuck out his hand and said, "Deal. But I will need my money first."

Bandy thought for a minute and told Richards to come to the house tonight and he would gladly pay him. Then, on second thought, he asked Richards if it was okay to pay him in gold. Richards smiled inwardly at the thought of George going to his stash of gold and not finding it there.

"Sure, George. What time should I come by?"

George looked at his watch, which showed it was about four p.m., and suggested Richards come over around seven. George would be sure that Claire was out of the house so they could have some privacy to make sure no one would be the wiser. Richards got up from the chair, finished his drink, and told Bandy that would be fine.

The call came just as Claire was about to open a bottle of her favorite wine. It was Richards telling her what he and George had planned. He then set up the double-cross.

"Call George at the office and tell him that an old girlfriend of yours was in Clarksville, just over the county line, and wanted to meet for drinks there at six. Trust me, he won't mind."

When George got the call from Claire, he couldn't believe his luck; not only would he not have to take Claire to dinner, he would have the house to himself to payoff Richards and to prepare for his own escape. Best of all, he wouldn't have to confront his slut wife.

The prenup she signed will protect me, he thought.

CHAPTER 55

THE PLAN

Hank and Simone sat in her hotel room, and after some small chit chat about the funeral, they decided to put together an all-encompassing effort to pin George Bandy to the mat for his entire illegal doings. The team showed up around five, and drinks and food were ordered in for everyone, as it was going to be a long night. Ritter was not going to end the meeting without a concrete plan to nab Bandy and the man they now believed to be a war deserter. Because of the new information regarding Evers, Hank had been able to get two more agents to fly in from DC to help round him up. In all, there were seven agents that had a combined total of almost a hundred years of field experience. The expanded team was confident they would succeed, and in fact some were almost giddy at the fact that this would be an easy task.

Based on his experience with chasing Ronald Evers, Hank knew the effort wasn't without great risk, and he expressed his feelings only to be chastised as being either too inexperienced or too ignorant of the power and expertise of the great FBI. Hank felt sorry for those that would be lost in the undertaking and only hoped that he would not be one of them.

Special Agent Simone Ritter stood and asked for quiet. Because of her stature, she was given the respect she expected. "Let me set this plan in motion by letting you all know that we have operatives undercover who will be acting as suppliers to Bandy and his thugs. They have already contacted him, and we plan to trap him in his quest to buy from our agents. The time frame is not yet set, but by end of day tomorrow, it should be in place. It's a large buy, and when we take him down, there will be serious charges against him that will put him away for a long time. If we can hook him to the killings of Sheriff Tate and Lacy Anderson, we could put him in the chair," she said, referencing the electric chair at the federal prison.

Antwan Delporto, the FBI agent that flew in to join the team, had with him enough heroin and marijuana to more than get an entire small city high all by himself. He explained that through various covert channels they had made contact with Bandy, though not by name. They had contacted him through a clandestine network of low-end buyers who led them to Bandy, and then they had made contact with him in order to sell him the contraband. Agent Delporto dubbed the operation *Last Call.*

Delporto had been chosen for the task because of his obvious ethnic background. His cover was that of a drug lord from Spain. The plan was to trap Bandy and anyone else they could during a daring midnight bust that would have all hands on deck. George had been under observation for some time, and it was plain for all to see that he indeed was the leader of the drug cartel in this area of the state.

"I have made first contact with his group and have been working with him to set up a big buy. If it happens the way we think it will, Bandy will be toast," Delporto said. "We have undercover personnel that are working hard to get this deal done, and within the next two to three days, we should have a time and a place set up. You all will be informed as things progress. Any questions?"

Delporto looked at the screen on his phone when it buzzed and recognized the number; it was George Bandy. The code words had been set, and Delporto answered with "Supermarket." He mouthed the word "Bandy" to the other agents.

"This is meat man. Is my order ready?" Bandy said. "It seems like we have everything we need to complete the purchase and would like to take delivery after midnight."

Delporto answered in the affirmative and asked where the delivery was to be made. George explained how to get to the old cabin on Smoke Mountain Road and said he would be there at three in the morning and abruptly hung up when he was told no problem. The agents thought it odd that he set the meeting place where a few weeks earlier there had been the raid where Sheriff Tate was killed.

George had made up his mind that he was getting out now, and he might as well have one more load of drugs to sell as he made plans to leave the country. His greed would be his downfall; he just didn't think that way. Delporto turned to Ritter and simply said, "Agent Ritter, I've got this." Ritter wasn't sure if she felt he was just a power-hungry jerk or if he just didn't care for the fact that she was, till he got here, running the team.

Huh, she thought, *and the prick didn't refer to me as Special Agent.* She was pissed!

CHAPTER 56

SURPRISE, SURPRISE

Claire was hiding in the basement family room when George came home from his meeting with Richards. She knew that George would be coming down to the lower level to open the safe room where he kept his gold. She had been down there many times with George because, like the egomaniac he was, he liked to keep Claire impressed with how much hidden wealth he had while at the same time making sure she understood that she needed to do his bidding if she wanted to continue sharing the wealth.

She seethed as she waited for George to bring Richards down to pay him, as she remembered a few times he made her undress and actually lay down on gold coins that he spread beneath her as he made her give him oral sex and a few times actually screwed her right there. What an egotistical prick he was, but at the same time, she didn't object because of the lifestyle she was afforded. When she heard the front door of the house open on the intercom, she glanced at the small screen that showed pictures from several cameras placed not only around the outside of the house but inside as well. George had the system installed a few years back when he used the basement as an office, which was before he purchased and restored the house downtown. It would not protect him tonight!

George entered the house, went straight to the bar, and made himself a drink. From the looks of the way he was walking, it was obvious to Claire that he had already had a few at the office. She wondered what else he had done at the office and wondered, as well, who with. She knew he was not loyal to her, not that she was to him, either. She had seen several of George's playthings and realized that as great as she thought she looked at her age they all had a certain something that she did not, at least anymore. She also knew that depended on who you asked. If one was to ask Kent Richards, there would be no questions about her abilities.

Claire watched as George sat on the couch and set his drink on the coffee table. She glanced at the clock on the wall and saw that it was six-thirty. Richards would be there in about half an hour. Claire would relish the occasion when George took his last breath; she wouldn't have the slightest emotion that would indicate they were man and wife. She remembered the way she was forced to sign that stupid prenup. When she disappeared with Richards and the gold, the prenup would make no difference. For a fleeting moment, she wished George wouldn't have to die, but it was very fleeting.

From her vantage point in the basement, Claire watched in dismay as George got off the couch, took another swig of whatever he was drinking, and went to the gun safe on the other side of the bar. He unlocked it and opened the door, carefully removing a revolver. She couldn't tell for sure, but she figured it to be loaded as George never thought an unloaded gun was much good in an emergency. He was right, and this for him was just that.

George sat back down on the couch and thought about his life and how he had managed to get this far without being caught, and if things went right tonight, he would be in Europe by this time tomorrow. With the wealth he was bringing to the party, he would have no problem replacing Claire, or for that matter perhaps two Claires. Then again, maybe the Scotch was giving him delusions of grandeur. He would find out soon enough.

He put the gun in the small of his back under the sport coat he had on when he heard the knock on the door. He still didn't trust Richards entirely, so the gun would come in handy if he needed it. Rather than getting up, he said rather loudly, "Come on in! The door is open, Kent."

Claire watched on the monitor as Richards entered the room and wished she had a way to warn him about the gun but thought that if Richards was that naïve she didn't need him that bad. With the money she would have, she could easily replace him at will no matter where she ended up. At that moment, she remembered that as bad as her experience was in the Bahamas those many years ago, that might just be a great place to start her new life.

Richards took one look at George and could see that this was going to be easier than he thought. George's eyes were a bit glassy, and his speech was a bit slurred.

"Hey, Richards, how ya doing tonight? All ready to deal?" George asked just a bit too loudly, indicating to Richards that George was half in the bag.

Richards responded, "I was born ready, George. Have you made up your mind exactly what you want me to do?"

"Sure did. I want you to get rid of Hank Maples, and if Ritter gets in the way, her too. How about I just double what I told you and you and I will disappear?"

"So to be clear, you will pay me forty grand to do Hank, and if Ritter is in the way, she gets it as well. Is that what you are saying? Because a few hours ago, you offered twenty."

George looked at Richards and shook his head as if to say yes then stuck out his hand to seal the deal. Richards took his hand, and before he shook it, he reminded George that he needed paid up front. He also reminded him he was paying in gold.

"No problem, follow me."

Bandy got up and headed to the stairs that led to the basement area. Claire watched on the monitor, and as she saw George and Richards come down the steps, she decided to confront George then and there. When he saw Claire, George stumbled down the last step and grabbed the handrail.

Drunk and stupid, Claire thought.

George looked first at Claire then back at Richards.

"What the fuck is going on here, Claire? I thought you were meeting friends for drinks."

Claire's eyes met his full on, and then she glanced at Richards and back at George.

"*Tsk tsk tsk*, George. You are a bigger fool than I thought you were. Did you really think you could walk out on me and leave me with nothing after all the bullshit I've put up with from you all these years? You must think I'm stupid."

George looked again at Richards, pointed at Claire, and shouted, "Fuck you, Claire. Richards has a surprise for you, you fucking whore!"

"Not so fast, you dumbass," she said. "If there is any surprise here, it's that Kent has one for you, not me."

George turned to Richards and said, "Okay, listen. There's another twenty thousand if you just kill her right now!"

Richards smiled and asked George to show him the money. George looked at Claire and said, "You think you can outwit me, bitch? Get ready to say goodbye to this life. May you rot in hell. Follow me, Richards. The gold is right behind this hidden panel."

George pulled a small remote much like a car door opener and pushed a button on it. The front of the panel started to move to the left. When it was fully opened, George pointed to the drawers in the back and one by one opened them only to find they were empty.

He realized then that he was indeed in big trouble. "Looks like your luck just ran out, asshole," Claire said, and as she did, she moved closer to Richards, who gave her a big hug, and just to piss off George, he kissed her full on the lips.

George knew he was doomed but wanted to take one last chance to save his life. He tried to explain that he had a deal to buy more drugs going down at three a.m. and if Richards would let him live, he would take him to the drop-off, buy the drugs, and then give them to Richards if only he would let him live.

Both Claire and Richards began to laugh at the sniveling, pathetic old man. George started to get down on his knees as if to beg for his life.

Claire had forgotten about the gun George had concealed behind his back. Before she could say anything, George had pulled out the revolver and got off one shot before Richards returned fire. Bandy had blood pouring out of his throat and started to fall the rest of the way down to the floor from his kneeling position. Claire's eyes widened, and she grabbed her chest with her right hand. When she pulled it away, it was full of blood. She had time to watch as Bandy crumpled the rest of the way down to the floor, and while she felt no pain, she did feel the life drain from her body. Claire couldn't stand anymore. Her knees buckled, and she started to grab at an imaginary object that she thought she saw that would keep her from falling. Her eyes betrayed her, and as she slumped to the floor and started to lose consciousness, her last thoughts were of the life she wanted, the life she thought she deserved, and, alas, the life she ended up with.

Richards looked at them both without remorse. In fact, he saw another opportunity. He would go to the old cabin and make the drug deal and take all of George's gold. He left George and Claire as they were in the basement of the house that had given them so much pride, and now it would become their graves. With a little imagination and a few turns of some gas valves in the kitchen, the bathroom, and the garage, the house went up in flames as Richards watched from the other side of the street. The deep blue flames ate up almost the entire house before Richards heard the wail of the sirens from the fire trucks that would ultimately be way too late to save any evidence that might give away any clues as to what had happened at the once lovely home.

Richards' work was almost done. There was still the matter of Hank Maples.

CHAPTER 57

LAST MAN STANDING

Richards walked away from the frantic scene and the screaming neighbors who were trying to interact with the fire department and the police that were on the streets forming a blockade around the tragic event. He walked now at a brisker pace to be sure he wouldn't be seen on the cameras of the news crews that had arrived and were setting up to take pictures for the evening news. He continued to think about the next few days and what he needed to do in order to finish what he started on the mission he embarked on several years ago, killing Maples.

Bandy had said the buy at the old cabin on Smoke Mountain Road was at three in the morning, and when Richards looked at his watch, it was already past midnight. Time was short, and he also needed to find Hank Maples to complete his quest.

Richards had been keeping a close eye on the FBI's movements and, of course, Hank Maples' whereabouts. He suspected that George Bandy's drug buy might have been another sting. So he staked out Tate's old office, where the agents had been working from, and watched as the FBI team came out and one agent put packages that looked like drugs into an SUV.

Word of the fire and the death of George and Claire Bandy had reached Ritter and her team. She promptly cancelled the sting operation, and Ritter sent Agent Delporto packing. "You and your drugs can go home now." She smiled. And that's just what Delporto did, under the watchful eye of Richards.

As he looked on, hoping to spot Hank Maples, Richards thought, as he had many times, that it seemed odd that so many others had died in his quest to get revenge. He wasn't sure how the end would go down, but he had to come up with a plan to try and get Maples away from the rest of the team to improve his odds for success. With Delporto and his agent gone, the odds had improved.

Richards now knew the drug buy at the cabin was set up to get George Bandy. He wondered whether the FBI had some notion of his connection to George. Was he the hunter and the hunted?

He watched into the night as the FBI team tore down the equipment they had brought in that made up their command headquarters in the hunt for the now-dead ringleader George Bandy.

The SUVs were loaded and the agents were preparing to leave town for the trip back to DC. Their charter was waiting for them, and the captain had called to say they had been given clearance to take off when ready. Ritter approached Hank and asked what he intended to do now that Bandy was dead.

"You know what I'm going to do. Why do you ask?" Hank answered. "I'm going after Evers. It's what I came here to do in the first place. I intend to find him and either bring him in or, if I get a chance, kill him. Deserting from the Army is one thing, but killing Lacy is quite another. It's personal now."

"What proof is there that Evers had anything to do with her death? What about Bandy? My money's on him as the perp," Ritter said. "If you go after him without proof, you put yourself at risk for legal trouble, but if you are hell bent on doing that, you can count me in to help you."

"I appreciate that, Special Agent, but you have a career to watch out for, and I wouldn't want you to jeopardize that for me, because there will more than likely be only one of two results: one, I kill him, or two, he kills me. I see no other way this ends!"

Ritter looked like she could stomp on rocks and crush them. "Listen up, asshole. It's not something you have a choice in. I either join you or I get the FBI and your precious USAIS command to come here and not just stop you but arrest you for insubordination. Evers is one evil fucker, and not that I think you can't handle him, but it never hurts to have an extra set of eyes, especially if those extra eyes are trained and have loaded weapons as well!"

Hank looked at her, and as she began to smile, he thought that she was more than likely right. After all, she did have something else that he had enjoyed before. So he just smiled back, stuck out his hand, and said simply, "Deal. Let's meet later and come up with a plan to trap him and get this over with ASAP."

"I have another idea," Ritter said. "Why not come over to my room and I'll explain? Be there at four."

Hank simply nodded. He arrived on time. The door was unlocked, and when he entered the lights were dimmed, the curtains closed, and Simone was on the couch with a bottle of white wine on the table with two glasses in front of her, wearing nothing but a smile.

CHAPTER 58

THE CHALLENGE

The streetlights were on when they were done with their *planning session*. Both were exhausted and slept most of the day in each other's arms. They were both starved and decided to get ready and go to Delany's for a bite to eat. As she was getting out of the shower, Ritter's phone buzzed. It was her team leader letting her know that the plane was about to take off; the captain wanted to leave in about twenty minutes and told him that if Ritter wasn't there, the plane would leave without her. "Thanks, but something has come up, and I'll not make that flight. Tell the captain that he has my permission to leave me here and I'll get another flight back to DC in a day or two. Have a safe trip. I'll see you in a few days." With that said, Simone and Hank finished dressing, called for a cab, and headed to Delany's for that late dinner they had talked about earlier.

From inside a rented truck, Evers had watched as the team left and now was outside the small hotel where he had followed Ritter and Hank. It was clear to him that because the rest of the team had left, the odds against him just got better. He thought he could handle six to one, but he knew he could handle two to one. After all, he not only knew all the dirty tricks to kill, but he knew how to use them as well. He would wait until the time seemed right and make his move.

He saw a cab pull up and the two of them quickly get in. He then followed them to Delany's.

Hank and Ritter ordered drinks, and the waitress left the menu. Hank had his usual Jack Daniels, and Simone ordered white wine. She told Hank that she never switched drinks once she started.

"So how do we get Evers to come out in the open so we can take him down?" she asked as if Hank was now the leader and had all the ideas.

"Not sure we have to have a plan other than to be seen. I think Evers is watching and waiting for the right time, or what he thinks is the right time. He has proved to be very good at being bad," Hank said, and Simone just smiled and played with her wine glass. "What's so funny, Special Agent?"

She continued to smile and said, "Funny to hear you say 'being bad.' Seems to me you are good at being *bad* as well."

Ritter ordered the filet, side salad, and baked potato, and Hank went with his standard, cheeseburger and fries, to which Ritter laughed and said he should eat better so he would have more stamina. "Besides, that dinner would be on the government tonight."

After another round of drinks, dinner was served, and the two famished souls ate like there would never be another meal, after which they each had another drink. Both felt drowsy but content.

"We should go before we get too inebriated. We got a killer watching us," Hank said.

The cab ride back to the hotel was quick, but during the short ride, they could barely keep their hands off one another. And when the hotel door closed behind them, the last thing on their minds was the coffee. It could wait while they could not!

Morning rolled around, and the two investigators turned lovers were awakened by Hank's phone vibrating from its resting point on the desk across from the bed. Hank was surprised by the call, because other than his commander, the only other person that knew his number was Lacy. He knew his commander would never call unless Hank had called him and left a message to call him back. Hank did not recognize the number on the screen but decided to answer it anyway.

"Morning, Hank. Did you and the FBI bitch sleep well last night? I hope so because it will be the last time you wake up. Consider yourself a dead man. And if your bitch agent gets in the way, you will both end up like Bandy and his fucking whore wife Claire. I'll be seeing you, but you won't be seeing me."

Just as Hank was about to say something, the line went dead. Simone could see the shock and stress on Hank's face as he clicked off his phone. She knew right away something was wrong.

"Was it the devil?" she asked. "You look terrified."

"Worse than the devil, Simone. That was Ronald Evers, and he just admitted that he killed George Bandy and Claire. He said I'm next, and if you get in the way, you, too. I guess, then, that's our plan. He seems to know what we do, when we do it, and where, so I guess we just let him take the lead and hope we are ready when the time comes," Hank said.

"Hank, I've been around this block before, and guys like Evers are so captivated with their own self-worth and narcissism, they often overlook the fact that they have failings. More often than not, they find that in the end their ego fails them, and they end up captured or for that matter in a case like this, dead."

CHAPTER 59

ALL WRONG

vers was making plans to kill Maples and at the same time putting together ideas on how to escape the country when he completed his sworn task. His experience in getting back into the United States from Vietnam with a new identity was serving him well now. Whatever he had become, he had learned how to grease palms and avoid detection, much like Crow had done. There was a part of him that was sorry for the way he had to end it with Crow, but it was a small part. Still, he had some regrets about that.

For their part, Hank and Ritter concluded that there was nothing to do now but wait for Evers to make his move. They knew that without the backing of their respective agencies, they were on their own, and it would be up to them to figure out what Evers had planned. USAIS had called Maples off the job because they knew it had become personal for him, and that more often than not led to bad results. He told them that he was returning to DC on the flight that left the next day, after he had received his communication from them. He just never got on the plane. Ritter likewise had told her handler back in DC that she was taking a few days off, too, another lie. The two of them then were out on the same limb, and they were determined to make the best of it, and whatever happened now would be off the record.

Evers watched and waited as Maples and his newfound partner seemed to go about their daily business like they had no care in the world. He was certain they were on guard, given his threatening phone call. His ego wouldn't let him simply ambush him and walk away; that would be too easy. He needed to look into Maples' eyes as he died so he would know the same pain that Evers had been feeling for years. He had time to be patient, but not a lot of it. His escape plane was set up to leave the country in three days.

It was pouring down rain, and Ritter and Maples went to Delany's Pub for early dinner. Ritter drove her FBI-issued SUV. Evers watched them leave the hotel and followed them to the pub but parked across the street at an angle so he wouldn't be seen.

Ritter pulled up to the crosswalk in front of Delany's and said, "No sense in both of us getting wet. Get out here. I'll park beside the building and come in the side door that opens to the parking lot."

Hank loved being taken care of by the lovely special agent, so he smiled and said, "Great. I'll get us a nice cozy table for two and meet you inside."

Hank got out and went quickly into Delany's, which was fairly empty at this early hour. *The dinner crowd must not come in until later*, Hank thought. He was shown to a nice table in the corner, and as the hostess left him with two menus, a waitress approached and offered to take a drink order. Hank ordered a Jack Daniels on the rocks for him and a white wine for Ritter, wanting to surprise her that he'd remembered from last time. He kept his eye on the side entrance so he could spot Simone and wave her down when she came in and looked for him.

She never came in.

He waited a minute or two then got up and went to the side door, looking for her ride. It was parked as she said, but she wasn't in it or in the parking lot, either. Thinking perhaps the side door was locked to patrons to keep patrons from entering and guessing she had to walk around the front to enter, Hank went to the front of the pub and expected to find Ritter damp and looking for him. She wasn't there, either. He thought to himself that Evers had to have something to do with the situation and feared he might just be using Simone as bait. He gave the hostess a twenty and rushed out the door.

Hank ran to the SUV. The driver's side window was smashed in, and there was what looked like blood on the fragments of glass on the seat, the floor, and on the windshield as well. On the seat was a plain piece of paper folded over with the word *MAPLES* on the front of it. Hank thought the worst, and when he opened it, his fears were realized when he read the simple message: *"You die or she does. Be at the old cabin Stone Mountain Road one hour. ALONE!"*

Hank's first thought was that he knew where the cabin was because there had been several incidents in that area that hadn't ended well. Hank also thought to include the local sheriff, and though he wasn't sure how they could help, he called in to the deputy on call and told him what was going down and to be ready to come to the Smoke Mountain Road cabin if he didn't call back in one hour.

"Roger that," the deputy whose name Hank didn't remember said and added, "How about we set up at the old turn-off just below the road to the cabin? That way if we're needed, we can be on site in less than two minutes."

"Sounds good, but don't come with lights and sirens on."

"Roger that."

Hank hopped in the SUV and headed out to the old cabin, which was about forty minutes away. The timing would be close, and for the sake of Simone, he needed be on time. He knew Evers would be a man of his word and would kill Ritter if Hank was late.

As Hank approached the turn-off to the cabin on Smoke Mountain Road, he pulled over to the side of the dirt road and backed the SUV into a large mound of overgrowth so the vehicle couldn't be seen. He had decided to walk the last half mile up the winding road so he could hopefully surprise Evers. Hank held his 9mm in his hand as he approached the south side of the cabin, which was now only about one hundred yards away. Dusk was approaching as Hank crept closer to the cabin. He looked at his watch. He still had about ten minutes left of the hour that Evers had given him; he would need to make the best of the last of those last few ticks of the clock.

It's quiet, almost too quiet, Hank thought. When he was within ten yards of the cabin, he saw a small amount of light coming from a window. He edged ever closer to see if he could catch a glimpse into the cabin through that window. Now on the porch, he was crouched under the window and could see Simone in a chair in the middle of the room. Her hands and arms were tied to the armrests and her legs were likewise tied to the legs of the chair. Her head was hanging down and bloody, as if she was dead, but Hank saw the rise and fall of her chest from breathing.

To his dismay, Evers wasn't visible in the room, at least from the vantage point where he was at the moment. Had he been able to see Evers, he had decided he would take a kill shot and get it over with fast. Hank knew, though, that Evers had to be close but out of sight.

He was frozen in time, and for the first time in his life, he was stumped as to what he needed to do. His hesitation was costly! Evers could have easily taken a kill shot. But instead, he charged Hank from the shrubs beside the house and in an instant had his strong hands around his throat. He all but lifted him off the ground and then, as if Hank weighed nothing, Evers threw him against the side of the cabin with such force that not only did his weapon go flying, but he felt ribs crack. His head hit the porch step, and the last thing he remembered before he passed out was Evers standing over him with a satisfied smile that turned to a sneer.

When he came around, he was in great pain from the broken ribs, and the welt on his head felt like it was the size of a golf ball. Blood was trickling down the side of his face and dripping onto his shirt. He was just as tied up as Ritter was. As his eyes cleared, he could see Evers sitting across from him and holding a gun in his lap. Ritter's head was still hanging down, but now he could see no movement of her chest from breathing as he had a few moments ago. He could tell she was dead.

"Too bad about your friend there. I guess I must have hit her harder than I thought when I smashed her car window. Such a waste of a pretty young thing, but sometimes things just don't work out the way you want," Evers snarled.

Before Hank could say anything, Evers pulled the gun up and shot Hank in the right knee. He passed out from the shock and had no idea how much time had lapsed when he woke up in more pain than before. When he regained a bit of strength, he jerked at his bindings but to no avail.

"You fucking traitor son of a bitch!" Hank shouted. "Too bad I wasn't a better shot back in 'Nam, and you and that fucking Hanger didn't die then!"

Evers started to laugh. "Yeah, and you're a fucking hero, you piece of shit. I've suffered all these years. Now it's your turn. How does it feel, Sergeant Maples? Feel like a fucking hero now?"

Hank remembered his call to the sheriff's office an hour or so ago and thought that surely the deputies had heard the gunshots and would be busting down the door at any moment to save his life. He just hoped they wouldn't be too late.

Evers' eyes turned dark. "Oh, and about the two deputies, they won't be here to help. Fact is, they won't be helping anyone anymore. Just me and you now, Maples, and odds are in a minute it will just be me."

What was left of any thoughts Maples had told him that he was about to cash in his chips, and a million thoughts ran through his mind. He wondered what things he could have changed in his life that wouldn't have led him to this place at this time. *Nothing*, he thought.

He felt a sense of calm come over him even though his heart was racing at a pace that would surely cause a stroke. He wished that would happen rather than from a bullet.

Evers watched as a pained smile grew on the bloodied face of his adversary.

"What's so funny, you stupid shit? Don't you know you're about to die?" Evers questioned, and as he did, Hank's smile, though faint, grew broader.

With effort he didn't know he had left, he raised his head and looked Evers in the eyes and said softly, "I know that I'm about to die, and I also know that your time will come, too. The difference is that I die an honorable man and at a time I know. You on the other hand will be hunted until someone finds you, and by the way, that might be friend or foe. You will not know the honor of having died for a great cause. You will die not having accomplished anything in this life that is worthwhile. And when you kill me, you will lose your purpose in life, and that in itself is a death sentence."

With a look of true hate, Evers said, "You speak of honor. What type of honor is it for you and your government to take thousands of young men like me, put them in countries far away from home, and exploit them?"

Without another word, Evers raised his gun and shot Hank Maples between the eyes. The force from the round that ended Hank Maples' life knocked over the chair that Hank was tied to, and Evers stood and looked down at the still-open eyes that seemed, even in death, to be defiant. As Evers crossed the room and left the cabin, his only thought was why he seemed to feel no satisfaction. He hoped when he got back to Vietnam, he'd find Quy and start a new life. He had his revenge, or did he?

ACKNOWLEDGMENTS

While there are any number of friends and family who have encouraged me to get this work finished (so I would quit bugging them to read and then re-read various sections as I worked through this process of writing my first novel), there is a person that I think I should give some credit to who got me interested in writing in the first place: Shaunna Goodhart. When she was the editor of the local newspaper in Circleville, Ohio, she recruited a number of local citizens to submit articles for publication in her paper, the *Circleville Herald*. I told her I would, I did, and I enjoyed it so much that when I retired, in 2018, I felt that I could indeed write a novel. And Barbara Siegelman, who first read the unedited story, gave me some valuable ideas.

My hope is that you as a reader will enjoy this fictional story that is based on some of my Vietnam experience, so at least something good will have come from that time in my life.

If you have comments, please feel free to reach out to me through my website: harryrubinauthor.com. I am working on a sequel, though it took three years to finish this work, and if I have that much time left on earth, that too may get done. So, if you have an interest in finding out what happened to Ronald Evers, let me know!

Thanks for reading!

CPSIA information can be obtained
at www.ICGtesting.com
Printed in the USA
LVHW092107050321
680706LV00041B/1598

9 781646 632855